# KISSED BY A COWBOY 1 & 2

## HEART OF OKLAHOMA

### LACY WILLIAMS

# KISSED BY A COWBOY

# PROLOGUE

## PROM NIGHT – TWELVE YEARS AGO

*This was a mistake.*

The words reverberated through seventeen-year-old Haley Carston's head. Pulsed painfully through her heart.

They even trembled in her hands.

The pale pink princess-style prom dress poufed around her. There was no other word to describe it other than *poufed*. She looked like a strawberry cupcake.

The girl staring back at her in Katie's full-length mirror looked like a stranger. Too much blush, too much mascara. Dark pink lipstick. How had she let her new friend talk her into this much makeup?

Because everyone *let* Katie. Katie was that kind of person. The shining star.

Nothing like *tag-along Haley*.

But that girl in the mirror—she was a stranger.

Except for the scared eyes. Those were all Haley.

After Katie had found out she wasn't planning to go to the senior prom, she'd promised to find Haley a date. And no one said no to Katie.

But who could she have found?

Haley's dad had dragged her to Redbud Trails, Oklahoma in the middle of her senior year, after a job he'd been chasing hadn't panned out. They'd planned to leave after a few weeks, but Haley's Aunt Matilda had seen how unhappy she was at the prospect of moving again and offered to let her stay until her first semester of college.

Haley had expected to hate the minuscule high school, graduating class of a whole dozen. She'd never imagined she'd fit in, figuring she'd stick out like the outsider she was.

Instead, she'd found an immediate friend in Katie, who'd taken Haley under her wing and drawn her into her circle of friends—the popular kids—and made Haley forget that she hadn't been born and raised in small-town Oklahoma.

Most of the time.

Tonight, she felt like a silk flower in a room full

of hothouse roses. Pretending she was one of the crowd but woefully inadequate.

The three-inch pumps that matched the dress were already pinching her toes. She wobbled into the hallway and hesitated outside Katie's bedroom doorway. How in the world was she going to get to the first floor without tumbling down them?

"What are we waiting for?" Haley recognized the complaining male voice wafting up from the living room—Katie's boyfriend-of-the-month, Ronald Walker. Katie had commented more than once about how fine they would look in their prom pictures together. Haley thought maybe that was the only reason her friend was dating the jock and half-expected a breakup soon after tonight.

"Haley will be down in a minute," Katie said.

Showtime.

There were other voices laughing and talking. Katie had convinced the group to meet up at the Michaels' farm and carpool. Which meant more people to see Haley descend and face whatever sap Katie had found for her, some guy who felt sorry enough for Haley to be her date.

Her feet didn't want to move. But she was afraid Katie would come upstairs looking for her if she didn't go. She took the first step and let her momentum carry her down, down...

Voices got louder. It sounded like Katie had a crowd of friends in the living room.

"Maddox, heads up!"

When she heard the name, Haley lifted her gaze from the stairs, and she stumbled on the last step. She barely registered the projectile flying toward her until it *whacked* the back of her shoulder. Her foot caught in the long dress, and she tilted precariously.

A strong pair of hands caught her waist and steadied her.

And a kid-sized play football fell to the floor.

"Sorry," Katie's younger brother Justin, a freshman, muttered from somewhere off to the side.

Haley looked up . . . and up . . . and up into the strong-jawed face of Maddox Michaels, Katie's older brother.

Who should've been in jeans and a Stetson but instead was wearing a smart black suit and white shirt and black tie...

No. Oh no.

"Great, we're all here!" Katie sang out. "Let's have mom do her three hundred pictures so we can go."

Maddox let go of Haley's waist, but only after he made sure she was steady in the uncomfortable heels. "All right?" he asked easily.

She nodded dumbly, her cheeks burning hotter than the face of the sun. She'd only met Maddox twice before, and she'd found herself tongue-tied both times.

He was *handsome*. A *college guy*.

And she couldn't even stutter out a sentence!

"I think this belongs to you." He presented her with a simple wrist corsage of white roses. His fingers were hot on her wrist as he slipped it over her hand.

"Oh, um..." *Thank you.* How hard would that have been to say? But she only had one thought blaring through her brain. *Find Katie!*

She excused herself—had she even said *pardon me?*—and moved faster than the shoes should have allowed, pushing through the other bodies crowding the room. There Katie was, coming out of the kitchen. Haley took her friend's arm and ducked back into the brightly-lit room.

"I can't go to *prom* with *your brother*," she hissed.

Katie patted her hand, looking over Haley's shoulder back into the other room. "Look, I know he's an old curmudgeon..."

*Curmudgeon?* Was Katie insane? Her brother was...was amazing. Sure, he occasionally got irritated with Katie's wild schemes, but then, who wouldn't?

He'd just finished his freshman year on a football scholarship—quarterback, no less. And there was talk that a Division I team wanted to recruit him. He was that good.

And that far out of her league. What would she even say to him? Had Katie lost her ever-lovin' mind?

Katie's smile turned apologetic. "But he was the only one..."

...*who would go with you.*

Her friend didn't have to finish the sentence. The words Katie didn't say hurt just the same.

"Look, I don't have to go to prom," Haley whispered frantically. "I can just go home, and then he won't have to pretend to be my date."

"Quit worrying." Katie waved her hand like she was brushing away a gnat. "Everything will be fine. Everyone will be so focused on him, they won't even notice you."

Great.

And Katie was right.

Against her better judgment, Haley squeezed into the suburban Ronald had borrowed from his mom. She would've pressed up against the window but her voluminous skirt prevented her from scooting far enough in. Her face burned as Maddox calmly settled his lanky body beside her, one long leg pressing into the pink layers.

His shoulders were so wide he had to rest his arm behind her on the seat.

It took all her energy to keep from falling into him as Ronald showed off for the guys, speeding around corners until Haley thought she might get carsick. By the time they got to the banquet hall, her whole body ached from tension, and she hadn't danced a single song yet.

Maddox helped her out of the vehicle, and within seconds, they found themselves surrounded by guys offering high-fives and talking about the last games of the season. Girls flirted with him as if Haley weren't even there.

She couldn't believe Katie had done this to her.

Maddox wanted to kill his sister.

Not for the date. He'd met Haley a couple times before, and she seemed all right. Maybe a little shy, but not starstruck like a lot of the other high school kids.

Tonight was supposed to be three or four hours hanging out with Haley and his sister's friends. Home by midnight. No big deal.

But he hadn't counted on the other kids. They followed him around all night until he felt like a celebrity trying to avoid the paparazzi.

9

About halfway through the evening, he finally spotted a patch of daylight in the crowd and broke into the open field. Out of the decorated banquet room. All the way outside. There was a little church next door with a small playground and he made a beeline for it like he had a linebacker on his tail.

He probably shouldn't have pulled his date out with him. It had been sheer reflex to grab her hand when he'd made his escape.

But now that they were alone, he had second thoughts and dropped her hand. Maybe he should've left her in there with her friends. She was so quiet— it made her seem more mature or something—he kept forgetting she was a year younger than him.

The cool night air felt good against his hot face, but he still couldn't breathe. He loosened his tie, sticking a finger down his collar to try and alleviate the choking sensation.

Everyone's expectations were stifling. Even his mother! He remembered her whispered words before he'd left the house that night. *"Just don't get her pregnant—you don't want to ruin your life."* How embarrassing, and really, did his own mother not know him better than that? And what about ruining *Haley's life*? His mom didn't seem to have spared a thought for Haley at all.

He should be used to the pressure. After his dad

drank himself to death when Maddox had been fourteen, she'd started calling him *man of the house*. He'd worked early mornings before practice and into the night, keeping the farm out of bankruptcy after his dad had almost lost it all.

And now that there was a hint of fame on the horizon, his mom had become obsessed with Maddox's football career.

The expectations wore on him.

Football season didn't start for months, but he already felt like he was about to be blitzed.

Even so, he should probably suck it up and be sociable for another hour or so, until they could get out of here. He looked up.

It was full dark out, but an outside light on the corner of the building illuminated Haley. She was watching him, her lower lip caught between her teeth.

"Sorry," he said.

She folded her arms around her middle and shrugged. Her dress was pretty, but she seemed uncomfortable. With him, or with the situation?

He nodded toward the banquet hall they'd come from. "I didn't realize it was going to turn into such a zoo."

She shrugged again. She was so *quiet*, he couldn't get a read on her.

"You're not having fun," he guessed. He turned slightly away and ran a hand through his hair. "This was a bad idea." He gave the empty merry-go-round a shove, sending it spinning. "This is probably a nightmare compared to how you imagined your senior prom."

"I never imagined it," she whispered.

He barely heard her over the metal squeaking as the merry-go-round wound down.

"Why not?" He glanced back at her.

She looked into the distance, still clutching her elbows with both hands. "My dad and I move around a lot. This is my fifth school in three years."

"So...?"

"So it's hard for me to make friends. I never planned on *going* to senior prom, but Katie..."

"Katie," he agreed, trying for lighthearted.

Instead of smiling, she turned her face to the side. "Sorry you got stuck with me," she muttered.

"I'm not." He probably surprised them both with the statement. "Unlike most everybody else, I know how to say *no* to Katie."

In the dim light he could see her luminous hazel eyes. Maybe they were filled with hope, with expectations, but somehow, she didn't make his chest tighten up like all the other kids did.

"We didn't get to dance," he said. When he

reached for her, she stepped into his arms. He'd expected her to be hesitant, and maybe she was, but somehow, she fit there, in his arms. His heart pounded like he was about to throw a fourth and goal. He shuffled his feet, barely moving to the muffled notes audible even though they were outdoors and away from the dance.

What was going on here?

"I'm sorry about all of...them," he finished lamely. All the fanfare, the kids following him around all night. They'd all heard about State sniffing around after the season wrapped. If he was recruited, there was a chance he'd been seen by the pro scouts.

His mother, his friends—heck, the whole town had stars in their eyes.

"I don't think they get it," she said softly, her words a puff of warmth against his neck. "Only like one percent of all college players get drafted to the NFL."

She peered up at him, biting her lip again like maybe she shouldn't have said that.

"You're a football fan?"

"Not really. My dad."

He was having a hard time concentrating on talking. He didn't want to think about all those *expectations*. Not right now.

She said softly, "It's a lot of hard work."

Looking down on her, he thought about the kind of work it would take to get to know someone like Haley. She wasn't the typical girl, falling all over herself to get him to like her. She was...real, somehow.

"I'm not afraid of hard work."

He saw goosebumps rise along the slope of her shoulders, felt her shiver through his hands at her waist.

"Do you have a backup plan?" she asked. "In case the football thing doesn't pan out?"

Here was another reason to like Haley. Her smarts. Once, he'd overheard her coaching Katie before a big test. Now that he knew she had moved from school to school, it was even more impressive that she could keep up with the assigned work.

He pulled her to his chest, and her face tipped up to his.

He thought he should probably kiss her.

When their lips were only an inch apart, she leaned back. "I don't want you to kiss me, just because Katie forced you to be my date."

And that's the moment he fell a little bit in love with Haley Carston.

"All right."

And he bent his head to kiss her anyway.

# CHAPTER 1

*H*aley Carston walked out of the bank and into the mid-June day. Summer was coming to western Oklahoma, and she knew better than to expect this mild weather to last.

She clutched the manila folder in one hand. The power of attorney for her aunt was a sign that everything was changing—and Haley didn't want it to. But she didn't get a choice. Life was like that sometimes —which she knew better than anyone.

The gilded glass door locked behind her with a decisive click. Haley had been the last customer of the day, and her business had taken longer than she'd wanted. No doubt the bank employees were in a rush to get home.

It shouldn't have taken nearly so long, but several of the employees had wandered into the bank manager's office to greet her like the old friend that she wasn't.

She'd only been back in Redbud Trails, Oklahoma, for a week, but the small town seemed to have a long memory. Everyone remembered her as *Katie Michaels' tag-along,* even though it had been over a decade since she'd left for college and stayed in Oklahoma City. She'd already lost count of the times she'd heard someone say, *"You used to run around with the Michaels girl."*

She squinted in the afternoon sunlight. Her memories of Katie were like a giant fist squeezing her insides and twisting. Haley had worked hard during college to shed the perpetual shyness that had followed her to the state university. But she'd never forgotten her best friend. Katie was a light that had shone too brightly—and burned out too quickly.

Just like Aunt Matilda. Haley's aunt had been diagnosed with inoperable cancer and wouldn't last the summer. One thing Haley had learned from growing up the way she had was you didn't get that time back. Her boss had granted her a leave of absence, and she arrived in Redbud Trails the next day.

Aunt Matilda needed her. And her aunt had been there for Haley through the dark days after Paul had walked away. Haley would stay by her aunt's side until the end.

Even if it was hard.

She paused to take a breath and admire the picturesque square in front of the bank. It had always been her favorite place in this town. Just as she was turning away, a small voice cried out, "Wait!"

A young girl rode up on a bicycle, dark pigtails flying out behind her, red-faced and huffing, her forehead slick with sweat. She hopped off the bike before it had even stopped rolling. She didn't even glance at Haley but ran up to the glass door and banged on it. Her purple backpack bounced with the force of her whacking.

"Please—" the girl gasped. She sounded near tears.

And the bank was most definitely closed.

"Honey," Haley said, "I don't think they're going to open for you."

The girl just banged harder. Stubborn.

"They c-can't be closed. I need to talk to a loan officer. I have to show them!"

What was the girl so upset about? Haley looked

for a parent, figuring that *someone* must be responsible for her. The girl looked about ten, but that was still too young to be in town, alone.

But no one was around.

"Hey." Haley approached the girl and put her hand on her shoulder.

The insistent banging finally stopped. The girl's head and shoulders drooped. She sniffled and rubbed a hand beneath her eyes, still looking down.

"Can I help you, hon?" Haley asked.

The little girl looked up, giving Haley her first good look at the turned-up tip of her nose, splash of freckles, and blue eyes. Her heart nearly stopped. The girl was a near-carbon copy of Katie. Down to the thick, curling eyelashes that Haley had been so jealous of back then.

She might've been the image of her mother, but the hesitant wariness in her gaze was all her Uncle Maddox. Haley's insides dipped at the single thought of the man she hadn't seen in over a decade.

"You're Livy, right? Livy Michaels?" Haley asked. "I'm Haley Carston."

The girl didn't react to Haley's name. Haley had rarely visited Redbud Trails after she'd entered college. Aunt Matilda had mostly opted to come down to the city. And Haley doubted Livy's uncle had ever mentioned her.

"Nobody calls me that," the girl said, pulling away and crossing her arms.

"Oh. Sorry. Olivia." Haley smiled, trying to show that she was a friend. She'd heard Katie call her the nickname once, right after Olivia had been born. Maybe the pet name hadn't stuck. Because Katie hadn't been around to use it.

"You look like your mother."

The softly-spoken statement did not gain Haley any points with Olivia, who watched her with slightly-narrowed eyes.

And there was still no parental figure in sight. "Is your uncle...?"

Olivia's expression changed to slightly-chagrined. "Um... I told Uncle Justin I was riding my bike."

*To town?* Haley's suspicions rose. She knew Maddox's mother had passed and had heard Maddox had custody of the little girl. Maybe Justin was watching her this afternoon.

"I really need to talk to a banker," Olivia said again, voice gone tiny. "It's important."

No one had even come to the door to see what all the banging was about. If Haley had to guess, the bank tellers and manager might've already left by a back exit.

"I don't think that's going to happen tonight. What about your uncle?"

Olivia looked away. "He's...um...he's on his way."

A likely story. "Can I give you a ride somewhere? Or walk with you...?"

Olivia's face scrunched. "I'm not supposed to ride with people I don't know."

Haley bit the inside of her lip, thinking. She couldn't just leave an eleven-year-old alone here, not knowing when one of Olivia's uncles might appear.

"Hmm. Well, you might not know me, but you probably know my aunt. Matilda Patterson."

The girl's face brightened. "Everyone knows Mrs. Matilda."

It was so bittersweet. Not many knew about her aunt's illness, and Haley's voice was soft when she answered the girl. "I know Aunt Matilda would love to see you. We can call your uncle and make sure it's all right. He can pick you up there."

The tip of Olivia's ears went pink. She turned her face to the ground.

Haley hated to be the bad guy but, "He's probably worried sick. I assume he has a cell phone...?" She fished her phone out of her purse and waited for Olivia to give her the number.

"Honey?"

Finally, Olivia rattled off a number, but when a

gruff male voice answered with a curt, "Yeah?" Haley's heart pounded in her throat and ears.

The man on the line wasn't Justin.

It was Maddox.

"M-Maddox?" Oh, Haley hated the stutter that slipped into her voice.

There was a pause. Then a gruff, "Who is this?"

Looking up with an expression so like her mother's, Olivia's lower lip stuck out the slightest bit, her eyes pleading for Haley's understanding. Or help. How many times had Katie used that very look on Haley?

And apparently, it still worked.

Haley forced a polite, cheerful note into her voice, the same note she reserved for her coworkers back in Oklahoma City. "This is Haley Carston."

She didn't exactly expect a warm welcome, maybe more of a *what do you want,* given how they'd left things, but he was completely silent. She could hear the rumble of an engine, muffled like he was in the cab of a truck. Maybe he really was on his way.

"I'm in town for awhile, and I ran into your niece outside the Redbud Trails Bank. I wanted to see if she could come over to Aunt Matilda's with me until you or Justin can come pick her up."

"She's in town? Alone?" he barked. And she recognized the worry beneath the gruffness.

Olivia watched, clutching her hands together in front of her.

"Mmhmm," Haley said, her tone unnaturally bright.

He muttered under his breath. She thought it might've been something derogatory toward his brother, but she couldn't be sure.

"Justin can't drive," he said. "And I'm on my way home, but I'm probably an hour out of town."

"Well, Aunt Matilda and I would love to have Olivia over," Haley said.

He hesitated. "Are you sure?"

"Of course."

"I'll be there as soon as I can."

MADDOX MICHAELS STOOD on the porch of the little Patterson cottage and braced his hand on the door-frame, letting his head hang low.

One of the large dining room windows was open a few inches, and he could hear Olivia chattering from somewhere in the house. Relief swamped him. She was okay.

He was going to kill his brother. Justin was supposed to have been *watching* her.

It was probably an act of mercy that Haley had found his niece. Maddox was working for a custom harvester, trading shifts with another guy who had a new baby at home. The crew would travel all summer, running combines and a grain cart. Dave needed the extra income but didn't want to miss time with his new baby, and with Justin incapacitated, Maddox needed to be home more, too. Right now, they were working in southern Oklahoma, but they would also travel up through Kansas and Colorado and who knew where else. Maddox didn't like the travel, but he needed the money, and splitting the time on the crew seemed to be working for both of them.

Until now.

Coming face-to-face with Haley was the last thing he wanted to do when he was feeling exhausted and beat-down. How in the world had Olivia gotten to town?

In his peripheral vision, he caught sight of the dusty pink bike leaning against the front of the truck parked beneath the carport, and the muscles in his neck and shoulders tightened. His hand slipped down the doorframe.

No. Olivia wouldn't have ridden her bike into town alone. It was three and a quarter miles to the bank.

Justin was a dead man.

The door opened before he was ready, and he

looked up. Slowly. His Stetson moved with his head, revealing her inch-by-inch.

But it didn't soften the blow of seeing her.

Her feet were bare beneath hip-hugging jeans, and she wore some kind of soft, flowy blouse. Her auburn hair was shorter, curling around her face.

And her brown eyes were as soft as he remembered.

She reached out and touched his forearm, and that's when he realized he'd leaned his palm against the doorbell. The buzzer had been sounding consistently. Annoyingly.

"Sorry."

"It's okay," she said. "Hi."

"Hi."

She was the same as she had been. That smile. Half shy and half knowing, and his gut twisted like he was nineteen again.

"You look good," she said softly.

He knew what he looked like. Older. Worry creases around his eyes. Covered in dust and wrinkled, like he'd slept in his truck. Which he had.

"You too." It was such an inane comment, and *good* didn't even come close to describing her. He needed to get out of here before he made more of a fool of himself.

"Can you send Olivia out? Is she okay?"

Haley's expression softened. "She's amazing. She's helping me cook supper. C'mon in."

He shouldn't. She must've seen his hesitation, because she paused on the threshold. "If you want to stay, Matilda and I would love to have you for supper. Either way, there's something I'd like to talk to you about."

He nodded. He swung his tired body into motion and stepped inside. Ahead and off to the left was the quaint, antiquey living room.

"Are you limping?" she asked.

He took off his hat, ran a hand through his brown curls, damp from sweating beneath the hat brim. The A/C on his pickup wasn't the best, but there was no money to fix it right now.

"Just tired. I've been out of town." His joints had gotten stiff sitting in his truck for hours. "I've picked up a job working with a harvest crew."

"Oh. So you have to travel a lot?"

"Yeah, a few days at a time. The farm's doing good though." If he could just keep ahead of his creditors. "Since Katie and my mom passed, it's just been me, Justin, and Olivia."

He tapped his hat against his leg. Nervous. And rambling. But seeing her again, after all this time... all his feelings came rushing back, like they'd been jostled loose by the vibrations of the combine.

He rubbed the back of his neck as he followed her through the dining room, where papers were strewn across the worn, wooden table. Past the dining room, he could see into a small kitchen.

That last summer, after Haley's senior prom, he'd followed Katie and Haley around like a safety chasing a wide receiver. He'd tried to be nonchalant about it, just show up wherever they were. He was pretty sure Katie had seen through him, but he didn't know if Haley had ever figured out how he felt about her.

And then Katie's pregnancy changed everything. Derailed his plans.

And heaped on another responsibility. Not that he regretted having charge of Olivia, but he'd only been twenty-one.

And speaking of.

"I should check on..." He nodded to the kitchen.

He passed by Haley, getting a whiff of something flowery.

Olivia caught sight of him and sent him a chagrined smile, not letting go of the spoon she held in one hand. "Hey, Uncle M."

Her subdued greeting was not lost on him, nothing like the chattering he'd heard before, through the open window.

She was safe. Thank God. He swallowed the

emotion that tightened his throat. "You're in trouble, you know that?"

"I'm sorry," Olivia whispered.

"What exactly were you thinking?"

"I needed to go to the bank."

He shook his head, didn't even know what to say. What she'd done was dangerous. Then he got a whiff and a glimpse of the pan she was tending. "What is that?"

She said something he didn't understand, her voice still soft and subdued.

"What?" he asked warily.

"Duck," answered Haley. "It's French."

He wasn't sure what to think about that, and it must've shown in his face, because Olivia giggled hesitantly.

"Uncle M is more of a steak and potatoes kind of guy," his niece offered.

He shrugged. It was true.

"Well, maybe it's a good thing you and I met," Haley told Olivia. "We can both appreciate the finer culinary arts."

He watched Olivia repeatedly scoop up the sauce in the pan and drizzle it over the duck. He'd never seen her do anything like that before. "Where did you learn to do that?"

"Food Network," Olivia said at the same time that Haley said, "Cooking classes."

The girls shared a smile, and the sight of it was like getting socked in the solar plexus. How long had it been since Olivia had smiled at him like that? How had his niece formed a connection with Haley in just an hour? Was it the cooking together? Or was it because they were both female?

He didn't know, and he wasn't sure he wanted to find out. "We've gotta head home, kid."

Olivia and Haley shared a glance, and he braced himself for the upcoming battle.

But it wasn't Olivia who begged him to stay.

"I know you've got places to be," Haley said. "But I want to talk to you for a minute."


THIS WAS A LITTLE SURREAL.

Haley couldn't believe that Maddox was really here. The first man who'd kissed her.

The man she'd dreamed would fall in love with her and want to marry her. At least she'd dreamed it until Katie's death had changed everything.

He followed her back into the dining room. She stopped on one side of the table and turned to see he'd paused on the opposite side. He faced her like she was the opposing team. His broad shoulders—

football shoulders—filled out the plain blue t-shirt, and his hair clung to his head after being under his cowboy hat all day.

But it was the shadows in his coffee-colored eyes that had her breath catching in her chest. This wasn't the confident *all of life ahead of him* Maddox that she remembered so vividly from that summer.

"Where's Matilda?" he asked with a glance toward the living room.

Tears rose in the back of her throat, but she coughed them away. "Napping," she said.

His eyes questioned her, and she shook her head. "She's been diagnosed with...cancer." The word was a knife in her throat. "The doctors say..." She took a breath. And still couldn't say it. "So I'm here."

She'd tried to keep the tears back, but the diagnosis and her aunt's impending decline were too close. She wrapped her arms around her waist and squeezed her eyes tightly closed.

Aunt Matilda's diagnosis had given Haley focus. Her aunt had been there when Haley had moved to Redbud Trails during senior year. She'd offered her niece a home when Haley's footloose father had been ready to move on. They'd talked on the phone every week since Haley had gone off to college. And she'd offered Haley emotional support when Haley's serious boyfriend Paul had broken things off.

Until now, the breakup and the distance in her relationship with her father had been the biggest problems in Haley's life. But they were minor compared to what Matilda was facing now. Haley was done wallowing in self-pity. When she got back to her life in Oklahoma City, she was moving on.

She held her breath until the impulse to cry passed.

"I'm real sorry to hear that," he said, and his voice was a little gruff. "Your aunt's a classy lady."

She half-laughed, half-hiccuped. "Yes, she is. Anyway"—she waved off the grief—"that's not what I want to talk to you about. Have you seen this?" She tapped the three-ring binder that Livy had been carrying in her backpack.

He came closer, caddy-corner to her at the edge of the table, and looked down at the computer-printed pages. He flipped one, then another, reading over the information slowly.

"What is this?" he asked.

"It's a business plan. It's Livy's."

He looked up sharply. Haley flushed a little, but wouldn't take the nickname back. Katie's daughter had wanted to be called Livy after they'd bonded over their love of cooking.

He looked toward the kitchen, where they could hear Livy humming a little tune.

"For what?" he asked, still looking toward his niece.

"Ice cream."

"She makes a lot of ice cream at home, different flavors, but... She wants to start a business?"

He looked at her with those unfathomable eyes. For a brief moment, an awareness swelled between them. A memory, a connection. Then he blinked, and it dissolved, leaving nothing in its place.

Haley shook away a tic of sadness. "She was trying to get to the bank to ask for a loan. She made up this business plan—it's actually very detailed. I'm surprised at how much work she's put into it. It's impressive for someone her age."

He furrowed his brow. "Shouldn't she want to be a cheerleader or play basketball? You know, do normal kid things?"

Haley winced but tried to cover it with a smile. "She is a normal little girl," she said softly, glancing over her shoulder to make sure Livy wasn't listening. How many times in her own childhood had Haley wanted to fit in with the other kids? And she hardly ever had.

"Some kids want those things," Haley said. "I think some kids know what they want to do with their lives. What did you want to do when you were Livy's age?"

"Play football." By the clenched jaw, she figured he regretted that statement. "I just don't get why she wants to make ice cream. There's already a chain in town."

"Not just ice cream. *Gourmet* ice cream."

He shook his head. "I don't get it."

"It's a different market than fast food," she explained gently.

He exhaled a long, slow sigh, shifting his feet. "How much?"

"Fifteen hundred dollars."

He ran his fingers through his hair. "You've got to be—"

"She's got a restaurant willing to sell her a used blast freezer at a great deal."

"A what?"

"It's a commercial-grade ice-cream maker."

He shook his head, looking down at the papers in the binder.

"I know it's a lot of money." Haley tapped the folder. "She's done some research. She's got great ideas, I think we could work up a marketing plan—"

"Thanks for encouraging her, but I can't afford something like this." He sounded sincere in his thanks, but also discouraged. He ran one hand against the back of his neck, fluffing the bottom of his slightly-too-long brown curls.

"I'd like to do more than encourage her."

He narrowed his eyes. "You want to give my niece fifteen hundred dollars?" he asked slowly. "Why?"

She shrugged. "I'm here for"—she drew a breath —"the summer, probably. I'd kind of like to go into business with her. Be her partner."

"Why?" he repeated.

*For Katie,* she wanted to say. And for him. For the dreams that had been lost to Katie's pregnancy and untimely death.

But mostly for Livy. When they'd been talking this afternoon, Haley had seen a glimpse of herself in the younger girl—a little girl hungry for love, for someone to believe in her.

"What if she fails? What if you lose all that money?"

"It's just money."

He looked at her like she'd said something crazy.

"Anyway, that's my problem, mine and Livy's."

He was softening. She could see it in the minute drop of his shoulders.

"Whatever happens, it'll be a learning experience for her," she offered.

"Teach her that life's hard," he muttered, looking back down at the table again.

"What if she doesn't fail?"

When he looked up at her, she saw the truth in

his gaze. This wasn't the same confident football star she'd known before. Maybe he didn't believe in his own dreams, anymore.

But Livy deserved her chance.

He glanced toward the kitchen again. From where she stood, Haley couldn't see Livy, but knew the girl could probably hear them. He seemed to have the same thought, because he lowered his voice. "If we do this, I'm not letting you take on the whole expense."

Her heart thumped loudly as she heard what he didn't say. "If...?"

He smiled. A sad little half-smile. More a turning up of one side of his mouth. "I shouldn't. This is crazy."

Maybe it *was* a little crazy. It felt more like one of Katie's old schemes than something the responsible, college-educated Haley would do.

But being here for her aunt, coming back to the place where Katie's life had ended too suddenly—both were reminders that sometimes, life didn't give you second chances.

Livy deserved to chase her dreams. Life was too short to waste it.

And Haley was determined Katie's daughter would have the chance. Even if it meant bumping into this handsome cowboy a few more times.

CHAPTER 2

*a* week later, Maddox still couldn't quite believe he'd agreed to Haley's wild scheme. Or that Haley had agreed to give his niece that kind of money.

He'd been gone on the harvest crew for four days, arriving home late last night. While he'd been gone, he'd relied on his cousin Ryan to help out and keep Justin in line. At least Olivia hadn't run away again.

After a short night's sleep, Maddox had been out with the cattle since dawn, starting with a headcount and checking fences. Since high school, he'd spent years building the farm back up after his old man had let things get so bad. Maddox had vowed he would never give up on life like his father had.

He'd just ridden his horse into the barn after cooling the animal down when he heard a car pull up in the drive between the house and the barn. Haley had promised to deliver the machine this evening. Olivia had mentioned it about ten times when he'd gone in for lunch earlier.

He stayed with his horse. He wasn't going to rush out to greet her like a high schooler on a first date. Hadn't he behaved like that enough that last summer? He'd stay here in the barn, even if his heart started pounding and his palms slicked with sweat.

Haley was here for Olivia. Maddox was in no shape to be getting interested in a woman. End of story.

Maddox brushed down the horse, keeping his feet planted right where they were. He thought about how she might smile if he went to greet her, how her curls would look in the fading light. He ground his teeth and ran the brush through the horse hair.

"Hey, Mad!" Ryan's voice rang out. His cousin had been over this afternoon, trying for the thousandth time to cheer up Justin. Or get his butt out of that recliner. Or both.

"Your new girlfriend is here!" Ryan called as Maddox tucked his horse back into its stall.

Maddox gave his horse one last pat. "She's not my girl—" He turned and stopped short. "Howdy, Haley."

Ryan jerked a thumb at her. "Followed me out here."

She peeked at him over Ryan's shoulder, grinning.

Something inside him responded, like his insides broke open or something equally corny. Really? He wasn't nineteen anymore.

"You're early," he groused.

She seemed to see right through him, her smile widening. "I couldn't wait any longer. I love ice cream."

"Livy's in the house."

She nodded but didn't seem in any kind of hurry to head that way. She glanced around the interior of the barn, and he followed her gaze, seeing it through her eyes. Ryan boarded a few horses here, and Maddox's four had stuck their heads over the stall doors, craning to see the owner of that female voice. Or maybe it just seemed that way to him.

He was proud of the place. It wasn't new, not by any stretch, but he'd replaced the roof a couple years ago, and it was clean and the animals were well-cared-for.

"You know, I think I only ever came out here once when I knew..." She paused and seemed to shake off the words "Back in high school. The place looks totally different."

"Good." He ran a much tighter ship than his father ever had, and it showed.

"Uh, the junior high principal called again," Ryan said as they headed toward the barn door.

"Something about Livy?" Haley asked.

Maddox shook his head. The man wanted Maddox to teach a class and coach the junior high football team. Mostly coach.

And Maddox might have considered it if he had the college degree everyone in Redbud Trails thought he did. The job wouldn't make him rich, but it would be better than traveling all summer, and it would be a steady supplement to the income they got from the cattle and small crops they were able to raise.

They left the barn behind and crossed the short field toward the house. He noticed the fifteen-year-old Ford she'd parked in the drive, her aunt's truck.

"How big is this ice cream thing?" he asked. He'd cleared a spot on the counter, but maybe he should have asked for dimensions before he agreed to house it in his kitchen.

"Well, it took three college guys to load it in my aunt's truck."

"Sounds like you need me, too." Ryan winked and flexed a bicep.

Maddox rolled his eyes. He might have been worried about Ryan moving in on Haley, except he knew his cousin was hung up on his high school crush. She'd joined the military and had been stationed overseas when she was injured. Now she was in a military hospital stateside. Ryan had been in love with her since high school. Never really looked at another woman.

Haley rounded the truck on the opposite side and threw back a brown tarp, revealing a plastic-wrapped stainless steel box about the size of an ice chest.

"That's it?" he asked. "The magic machine?" *Which cost so much money...*

"Yep. You guys got it?" She didn't wait for an answer. She opened the cab door and stuck her head inside the truck.

The machine was heavier than he thought it would be, and Ryan hopped in the truck bed to push it toward the edge.

When they hefted it between them, she met them carrying a cardboard box.

"What's that?" he asked.

"Early birthday gift for Olivia."

He opened his mouth to protest, but Ryan shifted the machine, jiggling it. "Mad, c'mon. This is heavy. Let's move."

He ground his back teeth and headed for the house.

She trailed them toward the porch steps, a couple steps behind.

"Do you really call him that?" she asked.

"Everyone else calls him Mad Dog. High school football nickname," Ryan grunted. "Why?"

"It seems like it would be a self-fulfilling prophecy. Like if you expect him to be *Mad*, he will be. Why not something like Joy or Sunshine?"

She said it with such a straight face that at first Maddox didn't catch that she was joking.

Ryan burst out laughing.

She quirked a smile at Maddox, and he almost missed the first step. He bobbled but caught himself with only a knock of one knee on the porch post.

"I suppose it is kind of a natural evolution from *Maddox*. But still...what's your middle name?"

Maddox wasn't saying.

"William," Ryan offered.

They finally cleared the stairs, and Maddox realized she would have to open the door for them. He moved forward, shoving the machine into his cousin's chest in retaliation for making fun of him.

Ryan's eyes danced.

"Hmm...you could've been a Will. Not a Billy," she

said as they carried the machine past her and through the living room and on into the kitchen.

"Why not shorten it to *Ox*?" he muttered. "That's what I feel like right now.".

Ryan froze, bringing the two of them up short, and looked at him over the top of the machine with an odd look on his face. Olivia, who was sitting on the far side of the counter, dropped her jaw.

Then his cousin laughed, a surprised burst of sound. "Did you just crack a joke?" Ryan asked.

Maddox ignored him as they maneuvered around the island to the space he'd cleared on the back counter. Finally, he put the machine down, arms aching, and turned to see Haley smiling down at the countertop.

"Who told a joke?" Justin asked, limping into the room, one crutch under his arm. He'd actually come out of his seclusion to watch the spectacle?

"Uncle M, I think," Olivia piped, her face scrunched in confusion.

The tips of Maddox's ears got hot. Had it really been such a long time since he'd made a wisecrack?

Luckily, Olivia's excitement seemed to distract his brother and cousin. She rushed to the machine, bumping past Maddox's elbow in the process. He overheard Haley murmur a soft 'hello' to his brother as she set her box down on the island counter.

41

Olivia started tugging at the plastic, but it wasn't coming off easy.

"Do you have some scissors? A box knife?" Haley asked.

"I'll do it," Ryan said cheerfully, digging in his jeans' pocket and coming up with a pocketknife. "Then I've got to get to the Reynolds'."

In moments, the plastic was shredded around the stainless steel box.

"It's awesome," Olivia breathed.

"It's a hunk of metal," Maddox argued. It pretty much was, with a small door on top and some buttons and a dispenser on the front.

Haley wrinkled her nose at him. "Just wait 'til you taste the magic that comes out of this baby." She started removing the plastic wrapping and crumpling the pieces between her hands.

"I'm out," said Ryan with a wave. He slipped through the back door, the girls chorusing "Bye," behind him.

Maddox leaned against the far counter and watched as Haley and Olivia made over the machine, Haley focusing as much on the girl as on the machine in front of them. Maddox wondered if she even remembered he and Justin were in the room. "We'll need to clean it first," she said.

Maddox was surprised his brother was still here.

Justin had been a bull rider until that accident. It was one thing to get thrown from a bull, but to be trampled by one, too? It had resulted in a career-ending injury—a fractured pelvis. Now, Justin was all but a hermit, limping around the house and battling depression.

But here he was, easing himself down into a kitchen chair and watching the two girls as they disassembled the guts of the machine and dunked them in a sinkful of hot, sudsy water.

"What flavor are you going to try first?" Haley asked.

"I was thinking about something fun, like this recipe I created for banana split." Olivia's voice sounded metallic as she leaned in close, her arm inside the machine as she extracted its guts.

"But then I thought for the first try, maybe I should go with something standard, like vanilla."

"Can't go wrong with a longstanding favorite," Haley said. She scrubbed one of the parts, then rinsed it and set it on a dishtowel to one side of the sink. She'd made herself right at home. She and Olivia were two of a kind, Olivia's dark curls at Haley's auburn shoulder, both of them washing up.

He'd thought she would drop off the machine and be in a hurry to leave. Apparently he'd been wrong.

And then she looked over her shoulder, right at him. "So what's for supper, boys?"

He hadn't thought she would stay. But Olivia's face was all lit up, and he found himself saying, "I can fire up the grill..."

"Uncle Justin makes a mean barbecued chicken," Olivia said, then sent an uncertain look over her shoulder, as if she might've blundered by saying so.

Justin had been so closed in his own little world since his injury, temper close to the surface and frequently boiling over.

Maddox had shouted louder than a coach from the sidelines after he'd let Olivia ride off to town the other day. The younger man hadn't even noticed she'd been gone, too dazed and drugged on pain meds.

But now Justin met Olivia's gaze squarely, his expression clear-eyed for the first time in a long time.

"If I can get a pretty girl to hold the platter for me, I'll give it a shot."

Haley laughed, drying her hands. She threw her arm around Livy's shoulders. "Do you think he was talking about you or me?"

She wasn't quite the shy girl he remembered. She'd matured, but her gentle spirit was still there. He watched as the girls shifted from the now drying equipment to Olivia's notebook and bent over it.

He could almost feel himself falling for her again.

But that was dangerous.

He wasn't the same boy he'd been back then, either. He was a college dropout whose dreams had been put on hold forever.

He didn't know how to dream anymore.

EVEN THOUGH JUSTIN flirted with Haley under the guise of teasing Livy, she knew he was harmless. There was something broken behind his eyes.

It was Maddox's sometimes-hot, sometimes-angsty gaze that she couldn't ignore.

It sent prickles up the back of her neck and made her fidgety as she and Olivia reassembled the blast freezer. At least she could pretend her fumbling was because the machine was new to them.

Finally, they got it back together.

"This is a great spot for it," she told Olivia. It really was. A wide swath of bare cabinet halfway between the stovetop and sink, with access to the island in the middle of the kitchen.

"Uncle Maddox moved some stuff around so it would fit."

"Oh, he did?"

Now that Olivia had mentioned it, the microwave was a newer model that didn't match the rest of the worn appliances. The microwave had been mounted above the stove, and freshly cut wood showed on the cabinets where he might've cut them to make it fit.

Haley flicked a gaze to Maddox. The tips of his ears had gone pink, just like Olivia's had the other day. An adorable shared family trait.

"Kitchen needed updating," he muttered beneath his breath. "Got to start the grill." He moved away, slipping out the back door.

Justin stayed, pushing himself slowly out of the chair and shuffling around the counter on his crutch. "Outta my way, cuties."

"But we have to start our base," Olivia protested. She was practically vibrating with excitement, bouncing on the balls of her feet.

"If you want my special chicken you've got to let me marinate it for a few minutes, Livy-Skivvy."

"Uncle Justin!" Olivia's token protest and giggle showed she wasn't too old yet for the silly nickname.

"I've got something for you first anyway," Haley said, drawing Olivia away.

A small alcove made a nice breakfast nook, and Haley well remembered sitting at the small, round table with Katie in the wee hours of the night, talking about boys. Dreaming about Maddox.

She shook away the memories and moved her box from the island to the table.

"You brought me something?" The hesitant hope in Olivia's voice pinched Haley's heart.

She sat down and motioned the girl next to her. Olivia stepped up to the table.

"The restaurant was liquidating, so I grabbed them for a great price. You've got to have the right tools, don't you?"

Olivia exclaimed over the stainless steel pans they could use to make an ice bath, the industrial whisk and strainer, and the two pots, all of which Haley had tucked into the cardboard box.

The restaurant owner had given it to Haley for a steep discount, happy to be rid of them.

"Here's the best part," Haley said. She took out the small white gift box she'd tucked in the bottom of the bigger cardboard box.

Olivia unfolded the lid almost reverently. "Is this...what I think it is?"

She took out the child-sized apron that Haley had sewn for her. White with vibrant red flowers all over, ruffled on the edges. Similar to the adult-sized one Olivia had worn at Aunt Matilda's last week, when they'd first bonded over their shared love of food.

And the most important part, in the center of the midsection, an embroidered logo. Olivia's ice cream logo.

The little girl was silent for a long moment, and Haley wondered if something was wrong, until Livy spun and threw her arms around Haley, burying her face against Haley's shoulder.

Haley blinked back the hot moisture that wanted to pool in her eyes. She hadn't meant to get emotional.

"Happy birthday," she whispered.

"Thank you, thank you!" Olivia came away, slipping the apron over her head and reaching behind to tie the bow. She danced over to her uncle at the counter. "Uncle Justin, look!"

He smiled his approval.

Olivia ran outside, calling, "Uncle Maddox..." her voice faded as the screen door slammed behind her.

And Haley was left alone with Maddox's younger brother.

She let her eyes skim around the room. It was much the same as she remembered, the pale green walls, the same cabinets and countertops. The womanly touches were gone. There was still a dishtowel hanging from a towel rack where Katie's mother had always kept it, but all of her knick-knacks were gone.

It was plain, but homey, too. Comfortable.

And then she had nothing else to look at but Justin. He continued working with the raw chicken breasts on the cutting board, but he must've sensed her perusal.

"Nice gift," he said. "Nice of you to give her the machine, too."

She couldn't tell from the sound of his voice whether he really thought it was nice, or he was being sarcastic.

She'd asked Aunt Matilda about him after Maddox's mention of his injury. But she didn't know if she should ask about his recovery or leave it alone.

"I'm excited to work with Livy," she said simply.

"It's not exactly a lemonade stand."

"You sound like Maddox," she said before she'd really thought about the words. The other night, Maddox had been more than concerned about Livy's venture. He'd been negative, though at least he hadn't said anything to the girl.

"I was sorry to hear about your accident."

"Wasn't an accident," he drawled. "Bull knew what it was doing when it stepped on me."

"Oh." What else to say to a remark like that? She listened to the scraping of the knife against the cutting board, the ticking of the clock on the far wall. What was taking Olivia so long?

She brightened her voice. "So what're you doing these days?"

He kept his focus on the chicken, but she saw his face crinkle in a smile. It wasn't a nice smile, more like a fierce baring of his teeth.

"That's the question, isn't it? And the answer is *nothing*. I sit around all day in my pop's old recliner and watch soap operas."

"Um..."

The waves of anger radiating off of him were almost palpable. But there was something deeper underneath. Desperation.

"Livy said you helped her with a school project. So that's something."

"Hmm. Well, maybe I could have a career tutoring kids. Oh, except I barely graduated high school."

She didn't know how to handle his anger and sarcasm. If he was one of her friends back in the city, she would be comfortable enough to offer an alternative. To say *something*.

"They have adult education scholarships," she said softly.

"What?" he barked.

She cleared her throat. "Scholarships," she forced

the word out louder. "You could go back to school. The state university isn't too far from here."

"Did you hear me say I barely made it out of high school?"

She shrugged. "Doesn't mean you wouldn't do all right now. Especially as an older student."

"I'm not *that* much older," he muttered to the chicken.

Finally, Maddox and Livy returned, the girl wearing her apron and chattering excitedly.

Maddox looked between Justin and Haley. Thankfully, he didn't say anything.

But she wasn't sure how long that could last.


"So...THANKS for bringing the freezer blaster thing out," Maddox said.

Haley laughed. "Blast freezer. You're welcome." She slipped out the Michaels' front door and down the porch steps, Maddox following.

The last bit of white light hung on the horizon as twilight deepened around them.

"The ice cream was...good," he said.

She glanced over at him, incredulous. She'd seen him palm a lightswitch as they exited the house, and now the porch light illuminated his faint smile and the day's growth of beard.

"Okay." His lips twitched. "It was better than good."

"It's incredible," she said. "And so is Livy."

She thought they had a real shot at making Livy's business a success. With Haley's education and her job as a marketing assistant back in Oklahoma City, and Livy's ingenuity, especially when it came to flavors, they had a chance.

He followed her to the truck, their shoes crunching in the gravel. She breathed in the cool country night air, nothing like the urban scents she was accustomed to in Oklahoma City.

"It must be hard to be away from her, traveling so much."

It must be difficult, period, for a man raising a young girl and trying to be an emotional support for his brother.

Maddox said nothing.

He'd been friendly enough over supper, asking about Haley's job and life back in Oklahoma City. But now he was quiet, pensive.

Haley had seen Livy's breathless hope when she'd presented the ice cream to her uncle. She remembered having that same gut-clenching feeling toward her own father. Whether she'd been handing him her report card or a cookie she'd baked herself, she'd wanted her father's approval, needed the emotional connection.

Maddox had praised the ice cream. But Haley also remembered that Livy hadn't gone to her uncle with the business plan.

And Haley wanted Livy to have that special connection with her uncle.

"I would have loved a childhood like this," she said, too vulnerable to look him in the face. She stared instead at the stars above the roof of the barn.

He snorted. "What, growing up with two bachelors?"

"Growing up with roots," she said softly.

He rested one palm on the top of the truck bed, and she leaned against the side and continued staring into the heavens. Another thing she missed living in the city—the bountiful stars.

"My dad and I moved around so much when I was growing up, I never felt like I belonged anywhere. You can give that to Livy. Roots."

"How come your dad didn't settle down?"

She shrugged. "He was always chasing...something. The next promotion. A different job..."

She breathed in deeply. "At first, I let myself get too attached to places. Found best friends. Settled into school. But I was never enough to make him stay. Or, my needs weren't..."

She felt it when he turned his head to look at her. A flare of heat hit her face.

"And I don't know why I'm telling you all this." She dusted off her hand on her jeans nervously and glanced at him. "I'm over it now. I have friends, good friends in Oklahoma City. I'm happy there. I'll be going back once Aunt Matilda..." She still couldn't finish the sentence.

"Good for you," he said. "I'm glad."

But he didn't say the same about himself. Why did he work so hard? Was he really happy on the farm, or did he think he didn't have options?

Instead of voicing those questions, Haley asked, "Why do you call her Olivia? In the hospital, I remember Katie calling her Livy."

He moved one arm, palm sliding along the side of the truck. "We don't talk about Katie much."

*Why not?* The words were on the tip of her tongue, but something zinged inside her. A warning, maybe?

His feet shifted, like he was uncomfortable. "Whatever your reason for doing this...helping Olivia... Just remember, she's a little girl who will still be here when you go back to the city."

He sounded like he thought Haley's presence was going to hurt the girl, but all she wanted was to help.

"If this is some kind of...I don't know...call back to Katie's memory—"

"It's not."

He shook his head, gripping the top of the truck bed. "I can't help remembering how you two were thick as thieves..."

*Tag-along.* His words doused ice water on her. She'd had a wonderful evening with Livy, cooking the first ice cream base and teasing Maddox...

And he still thought of her as Katie's tag-along, after all these years.

She didn't know what to say.

He seemed to understand her sudden uncertainty, because he went on. "Look, I'm just trying to protect my niece. I appreciate that you're trying to do something nice for her."

She waited for the *but.* And it came.

"But giving her that money...building up her dreams..."

"I'm not doing it for Katie. I'm doing it for Livy. We're partners."

Nearby, something rustled in the darkness against the side of the house. It moved, but she couldn't make out the form in the darkness. Whatever it was, it was big.

She thought Maddox was arguing with her, but her thundering heartbeat drowned out anything he might've said. The Thing padded closer, quiet in the darkness. Were those fangs, glimmering in the dim porch light?

She grabbed his arm, ducking between him and the truck, turning her shoulder away from the animal's hot breath against her side. Was it a Rottweiler? Or just a huge mutt?

"Maddox," she hissed. Her breath came in gasps, fear overpowering her sense of propriety and personal space.

He brought his other arm down, caging her in. "What's the matter?"

"P-please tell me that's a friend."

He looked down, over the side of his arm, then tilted his chin back to her, the light from the corner of the house shining behind him and leaving his face in shadow. "You're still afraid of dogs?"

"I'm n-not afraid. Terrified."

He snorted.

"Git on, Emmie," he said softly.

The huge black dog sat, tail swishing audibly over the gravel of the drive. Its lips parted in a panting, doggie grin. The dim porch light showed that it lifted one paw in a polite shake.

"Git on," Maddox said again, his voice laced with humor.

The dog closed its mouth with a *huff* of air, stood, and sauntered off, fading into the darkness.

And then the man turned his gaze back on her. She looked up at Maddox in the moonlight, and her stomach swooped low, the same way it had when he'd held her on prom night all those years ago.

She could see the dark stubble of his days' growth of beard. His eyes were unreadable in the darkness.

If she wanted to, she could reach up and put her arms around his neck, stand on tiptoe...and claim the second kiss she'd been dreaming about for a dozen years.

But she wasn't seventeen anymore.

And he probably didn't think about her that way. They both had Olivia's best interests at heart.

And Haley wanted to protect her own heart, too.

His hands came to rest gently on her waist, but before he could push her away, Haley stepped out of the circle of his personal space. Her heart beat and pulsed in her throat, and it sounded a little like the taunt she always heard in her head. *Tag-along.*

"Thanks for supper. I had a fun time."

She thought he said *me too*, but she tucked herself in the cab of her truck and started the engine. She waved, smiling out the window into the dark so he wouldn't know how shaken the moment had left her.

She wasn't a little sheep any longer. She had her

own friends back in Oklahoma City. She wasn't *desperate* for company, no matter what he thought.

She would do what she said. She would see him peripherally while helping Olivia with her ice cream business. She would care for her aunt and mind her own business.

And they could both pretend that the near-embrace never happened.

MADDOX STOOD STARING after Haley's taillights long after they'd disappeared down the dirt drive, hands fisted loosely at his sides.

What had he been thinking? He'd *touched* her. She'd been so close, and he'd wanted her closer— wanted to find out if her lips still tasted like the ice cream they'd shared.

But the moment he'd given in to the urge and reached for her, she'd backed away.

He knew better than to reach. Hadn't his past taught him anything?

He didn't have time for any kind of relationship and didn't need Haley nosing into his business.

She wanted him to give Olivia roots. How was he supposed to do that, when he could barely keep them afloat? He wasn't doing that good a job keeping

Justin from sinking further into depression, and had a hard time keeping ahead of the medical bills.

He didn't know how to be a father to a little girl.

What did he have to give to Olivia? He was on the road or working dawn-to-dusk, just to make ends meet.

The expectations were too heavy. They had been ever since his teen years, when his mom had turned him into the man of the family. As if he could handle it, because no one else was there to do it. He'd just been a kid when his dad had died in a drunken stupor. He'd been a kid when they'd all expected him to become some kind of football star, and a kid when Katie had left him with a tiny bundle of pink. If love had been enough, he'd have been the best uncle in the world.

But what he'd learned was that his love and his desire to do the right thing weren't enough. He had to be better.

He was a mess, his thoughts churning with the burn in his gut, but no antacid would repair this mess. The last thing he needed was Haley around, tempting him to dream. If he had any brains at all, he'd tell Haley not to come to the house again, but...

She was good for Olivia. That was easy to see. She'd had all three of them, him, Olivia, and even

Justin for a few minutes, laughing in the kitchen like a real family.

And Olivia had soaked it up like a parched field in a rainstorm.

He was afraid he had, too.

When was the last time they'd felt like a family, not just individuals living in the same house?

He'd promised himself never to end up like his dad, always stuck in the could-have-beens. Maddox was making a life for Olivia, doing what he could.

It would have to be enough.

But what if it wasn't?

# CHAPTER 3

*T*hree weeks later, Maddox turned down the dirt lane toward home, fresh off of another four-day-stint on the harvest crew. He'd gotten up in the middle of the night and driven all morning to make it here by lunchtime.

The more he'd thought about the things Haley had revealed about her own childhood that night after supper, the more he'd been determined to prove that he could be the father-figure Olivia needed. He could do better than he had been doing. And being here today was a part of that.

Olivia and Haley had planned some elaborate birthday celebration. He thought they might've invited the entire elementary school. They were calling it a *business expense*, planning to do something with all the ice cream they'd made over the last few weeks.

Maddox had never seen so much of the sweet treat in his life. Olivia had been furiously mixing up batches, trying out new flavors with her old personal-sized ice cream maker, and hand-packing quart after quart in cardboard containers.

She'd even appropriated a deep freezer from a neighbor who wasn't using it any more. She already had that sucker half-full.

On one of his at-home breaks, he'd sat down with Olivia and talked about the three books her school had assigned as suggested summer reading. He'd asked about her friends, expecting her to duck his question. Instead, she'd chatted with him for almost an hour. Opened up to him, and all it had taken was him asking.

Haley had been at the house two Saturdays in a row, according to Justin. Maddox had been out with the crew both times.

During those long rides on the combine, he'd imagined his brother spending time with Haley. Justin had been known for his charming ways on the rodeo circuit. Unfortunately, thinking about the two together made Maddox need to pop an antacid. And he knew why.

Haley was special. Maddox had known it when she was seventeen, and he knew it now.

Knowing he was going to see her again today had him antsy and uncomfortable. And he had no business thinking about her like he was. He was barely keeping the farm afloat. Barely avoiding the creditors calling about the overdue medical bills.

Where he'd given up on his dreams, Haley had a fancy degree and no doubt fancy friends in the city. She even cooked fancy.

Even if he did find the guts to pursue her, what would she want with a farmer like him?

She was too good for him. The smartest thing to do would be to forget about her.

But Justin had seemed more grounded after her visits. Less stuck inside his own head. Maddox couldn't help wondering what passed between them.

He turned into the drive to see five farm trucks already parked in a snaking line.

"What the—?" He guided his truck around the outside, half-driving in the ditch so he could get to the house.

He would have sworn Olivia had told him the party would begin in the afternoon.

He parked his truck on the side of the barn, since apparently they were going to need most of the yard for guests.

"Mad, you're here!" Ryan's voice rang out, quickly followed by Olivia's, "Uncle Maddox!"

He braced one hand on his truck and caught Olivia with the other arm when she launched at him. She rubbed her face against his chest. "You made it!"

"I promised, didn't I?"

When she moved back, squealing with excitement, her face was shining. He was stiff and exhausted from driving most of the night, but it was worth it.

When she ran off, he looked up to see Haley standing right there, her eyes showing her surprise.

"Didn't think I'd make it, huh?" he asked.

"I'm glad you did." She seemed sincere, and his heart thumped once hard beneath his breastbone.

She led him to a picnic table that hadn't been in the yard before, beneath a tree that would shade him from some of the hot June sun. "Where'd this come from?" he asked.

"Neighbors," she answered. "Borrowed them."

That's when he saw there were ten tables arranged in a horseshoe.

And the yard had been mowed. "Who mowed?"

"Your brother." She nodded toward the row of trucks, where not only was Justin outdoors, he was leaning on his crutch, talking to old man Simpson. The grocer had been a friend of their mom's and

Maddox guessed he had delivered one of the picnic tables.

It was the first time Maddox had seen Justin willingly engage with someone outside their family circle since his fall.

Haley was still talking. "He said, and I quote, *'I can drag along behind the push-mower just as well as I can drag behind my crutch.'*"

He could imagine his brother saying that. Somehow, Haley had gotten him to mow the yard. He hated to think how, but the image of the two flirting with each other came unwelcome into his mind.

"I'm so glad you're here," Haley said, interrupting his thoughts. "I need your help. Have a seat."

In the next few minutes, Haley showed him how she wanted him to slice about thirty watermelons. It seemed like they were planning for a horde—he hoped Haley and Olivia weren't disappointed.

Haley tilted her head to the side, looking at him for a long moment. "You good?" Haley asked.

"Fine."

He didn't like the hot knot that had settled behind his sternum, thinking about her and Justin together. As he watched under the guise of cutting into one of the melons, she got some kind of magazine out of her aunt's truck. Haley marched up to his brother and slapped the book into his stomach.

His brother hugged her briefly around the shoulders, like he would've hugged Katie or their mom, and just kept on talking.

"They're just friends," Ryan said, voice low. Maddox hadn't heard him walk up.

He clapped a hand on Maddox's shoulder. "At first, I thought the same thing you were thinking, but she doesn't look at him the way she looks at you."

Maddox's stomach swooped at that thought. He'd been half in love with Haley when he'd known her as Katie's friend—and the woman she was now affected him just as powerfully.

Ryan had been checking on Justin and Olivia on the weekends Maddox had to be gone, so he must have known what he was talking about.

But it didn't make Maddox feel that much better.

Haley dashed by his table a little later and left a sampler plate of the ice cream. This had been their plan all along. Invite people for free ice cream.

He grabbed Olivia when she tried to skip by. After he'd complimented her on the ice cream, which was delicious, he asked. "How much is this costing?"

"Haley says you have to spend money to make money."

He just hoped they weren't spending too much.

He'd barely gotten started slicing the watermelons when cars began arriving. He smiled and greeted Olivia's guests, shocked at how many came. And kept coming. They seemed to arrive by the vanload. A lot of people he knew from church but hardly greeted on Sundays. People he'd gone to high school with that now had children in elementary school.

Olivia and Haley were in their element, whirling through the crowd, dispensing ice cream and chatting with everyone. He'd never seen either of them like this before. Haley had always been so shy. Apparently, she'd overcome that. And Olivia...watching Olivia was like seeing Katie alive again. It made his heart thump painfully.

Just a month before, his niece had been a sad little girl, defensive and lonely. Then she met Haley, and everything changed. Haley seemed to be exactly what Olivia needed. His little girl was blooming with Haley around. But how long was she going to stay?

HALEY COULDN'T BELIEVE IT. When Maddox had promised to be there, she'd envisioned comforting a very disappointed Olivia. Instead, Maddox had driven all night to be at Livy's party.

Her own father would never have done something like that.

She couldn't help it that her gaze kept straying to him during the hot afternoon. She saw plenty of folks greet him, many slapping him on the shoulder while he shook their hand.

She also saw the lines of stress around his mouth. But she didn't know why. Was it the money? Trying to run the farm while he supported Justin and Livy?

She'd barely seen him since their dinner together, but Livy had told her all about how they'd spent extra time together recently. The way Olivia talked about him, it was obvious the girl thought he hung the moon. And Justin had a grudging respect for him, even through his pain and depression.

Haley's high school crush had never completely gone away—and now it was back with a vengeance. She'd buried it under her busyness and college life. And that doomed relationship with Paul. Paul, who'd always made her feel like she wasn't good enough for him.

Watching Maddox now, she could see that he was still the same popular jock, but beneath that hard exterior lurked something darker. And she couldn't help wondering what it was.

By midafternoon, Haley needed a break. She'd been on her feet since this morning. She spotted a chance and plopped down on the bench beside Maddox, bumping his shoulder with hers. "Hey."

"Hey," he responded.

The top of the picnic table was covered with sticky juice from the watermelons and Haley was careful to keep clear of it.

Olivia showed no signs of fading. She spun from one person to the next, bubbly and grinning.

The little girl had been keeping count of the number of samples they'd handed out. They'd come up with the idea of purchasing small disposable condiment bowls and scooping samples into them. Each partygoer got a sampler plate, so they could try several different flavors.

And they'd printed quarter-sheet flyers listing the flavors and ordering instructions, which they'd handed out with each sample.

The response had been wonderful. People had marveled at all Livy had done, at the wonderful ice cream, and at the girl's ingenuity. Haley couldn't have been more pleased.

"She seems happy," Maddox said, voice low. "And I can't believe Justin was out here for awhile. What did you give him earlier?"

"Hmm?" She was so tired, she couldn't think straight.

"Earlier, I watched you hand him something. Looked like a magazine or—"

"College catalog. I've almost convinced him to enroll for the fall."

Maddox shifted to look into her face. "You're kidding."

He didn't seem particularly happy about it. The lines around his mouth had tightened even more.

"Hey, Katie's friend!" The voice came from a little cluster of folks near the back porch, and then a woman walked up to their table, waving off one of the last slices of watermelon that Maddox tried to slide across to her.

Haley froze, then forced a smile to her face. She recognized the woman from high school but couldn't remember her name, either. She shouldn't have been surprised to be called, "Katie's friend," even after all these years. Apparently, Haley would always be the *tag-along* in this town.

"Can I buy a quart today?" the woman asked.

"We hadn't planned to sell any until next week."

Maddox snorted. "Olivia's been running that machine night and day. I bet I could find a quart for you to take home. How much are you willing to pay for it?"

"You gonna auction off some ice cream, Mad Dog?" a man Haley didn't know asked, wandering closer from the crowd around the porch.

70

Maddox looked at Haley, something brewing behind his eyes.

He stood up, using the table for leverage, then bellowed, "Livy!"

The girl darted out of the crowd, beaming and wearing the apron Haley had made her.

She approached, and Maddox whispered something to her. She squealed and ran off to the kitchen.

While she was gone, Maddox started clearing off the picnic table. Haley helped, but when she asked what he was up to, he half-grinned and said nothing.

A few minutes later, Livy climbed on top of the picnic table, and Haley realized what Maddox and Livy had planned. They were auctioning off five quarts of the gourmet ice cream. Immediately, a crowd gathered around.

Olivia's eyes were shining, but Maddox looked slightly pained.

Maddox started, "Okay, we've got—" Olivia murmured something to him—"Chocolate covered strawberries, folks. Who'll give me fifteen bucks for this quart?"

It had been one of the most popular flavors of the day, and Haley wasn't surprised to see several hands go up.

Maddox got the bid up to thirty before his voice boomed, "Sold, to the gal in the yellow shirt." Within a few minutes, the rest of the quarts were auctioned and, with some cheesing up to the audience and Olivia chipping in about the ingredients she'd put into each different ice cream, sold for top dollar.

Handing out the prized ice cream, Olivia was bouncing with joy.

Haley watched from the edge of the yard, swelling with pride for Livy. All the work they'd put into this event had been worth it. And when Maddox's eyes met hers, that pride was replaced with something entirely different.

THE PARTY WAS WINDING down when Haley brought Maddox a bottle of water. He'd been sitting at the same table, though finally, he'd been left alone for a little while. He grabbed the water, twisted off the cap, and downed it. "Thanks."

"You looked thirsty."

He was wiping his mouth with his sleeve when Rob Shepherd, one of the loan officers from the bank, moseyed by.

"Got a neat little operation here," the man said. "I hope it pays off for you."

"It's all Livy," Haley said, sliding onto the bench beside him. Thank God she hadn't caught the man's undertones.

"Place is looking good, Michaels," he said. "I heard the medical bills might keep you from putting in that irrigation system you were talking about last winter."

Maddox could only imagine who he'd heard that from. Small-town gossip.

"Not this year," Maddox said, gritting a smile out.

The other man lifted one foot onto the bench opposite theirs and shot the breeze for another few minutes before moseying off.

"What was that about?" Haley asked.

He shrugged. "Folks around here have a long memory."

She nodded. He guessed she probably understood that, the way everyone still remembered her as Katie's friend.

She narrowed her eyes. "So...?"

"So some of them have been waiting for me to fail, just like my old man."

"Really?" She sounded surprised. "Back then, it seemed like they were all pulling for you."

"Not all of them."

She tilted her head to the side. "Are you sure you're not projecting?"

"What's that mean?" He shook his head. "Forget it." It was about time to find a trash bag. When he stood, she followed him.

"It means, are you sure *you* aren't the one worried about failing?"

She always did have a way of cutting to the heart of the matter.

He gritted his back teeth. He didn't want to talk about his pop with her. Didn't really want to think about the man—it was a waste of time.

She stopped him in the shade of the house with a soft hand on his sleeve. "No matter what anyone else says or thinks, you've got Livy—you've done a good thing."

The way she was looking at him, like she believed in him.... Suddenly, possibilities rose like a shimmering mirage.

He just didn't know if he had the strength to hope in possibilities any more.

# CHAPTER 4

*S*everal days after Olivia's birthday, Haley awoke feeling somehow...off, but she couldn't pinpoint why.

It wasn't until she was driving home after picking up some prescriptions for Aunt Matilda that she realized what day it was. The anniversary of the car accident that had killed Katie.

She was coasting past the small town cemetery when she saw a lone, small figure, huddled into herself. Livy.

Grief and hot disappointment surged through her.

Haley parked around the side, not wanting to interrupt the girl.

How could she have almost forgotten such an important day? And where were Livy's uncles?

She had her phone in her hand and dialed before she could talk herself out of it. It really wasn't her business. But she cared about Livy, too.

Maddox picked up on the first ring. "Haley?"

She should've held her tongue, but the words burst out before she could even think.

"How could you leave her alone today? Even if you couldn't bring her—"

"Olivia—?"

"Did she ride her bike to town again? I would've picked her up—"

"Haley—"

"She's at the cemetery, Maddox. By herself. Where are you?"

Her voice broke as she remembered standing alone at her mother's grave in a St. Louis cemetery, saying goodbye the day before Haley's father moved them across the country.

There was a long pause, as if he were waiting to see if she was really done railing at him.

Then, a quiet. "I'm here."

She scanned the area and saw his truck parked on the opposite side of the fence.

He lifted his hand from the steering wheel in a brief wave.

"She said she wanted to go alone."

The enormity of what she'd done crashed down

KISSED BY A COWBOY

on Haley. Not only had she ranted at him when he was most likely grieving too, but she'd accused him of neglecting Olivia again, this time when he didn't deserve it.

She squeezed her eyes closed, the hand that wasn't holding her phone squeezing on the steering wheel.

"I'm sorry," she whispered.

WHEN HALEY PULLED AROUND and parked beside his truck, Maddox wasn't surprised.

She was something of a pit bull beneath that friendly, smiling exterior.

He was starting to like it.

It made his voice gruff when she popped his door open.

She just looked at him for a long moment, silent and assessing.

"You okay?" Her soft-spoken question hit harder than he wanted to let on.

He looked out over the wrist he'd rested on the dash, squinting a little.

Then she shocked him by taking his other hand. Picked it right up off of his thigh, mashing it between both of her smaller, cool hands. Touching him again. Comforting him.

77

"I'm fine," he said.

But he wasn't. Not really. He'd spent all morning tiptoeing around Justin, who'd been more of a grump than usual.

His brother hadn't talked about the giant elephant in the room, their shared loss. So Maddox hadn't either.

Maddox's chest expanded, and he breathed out harshly.

But he didn't have time for more than that, because she was pulling him out of the truck. "What—?"

"Even if Livy told you she wanted to be alone, that's not what she needs."

He dug in his heels, unease bucking like an unbroken bronco.

She shook her head. "We've got to get you educated on woman-speak before Livy turns into a teenager."

She tugged him forward, and this time he went, mostly to save his wrist from being pulled out of socket.

He didn't know how to handle Olivia's grief. He didn't even know what to do with the hot ball lodged in his own gut.

He wasn't equipped to deal with this. Maybe he never would be.

But somehow... Having Haley at his side made the trek past all those other graves less daunting.

Olivia looked up at their approach, and the pain in her eyes nearly sent him to his knees. But she was dry-eyed, thank God.

Haley let go of his hand, and he felt the loss intensely, but she wrapped both arms around Olivia's shoulders.

The sight of them together, like mother and daughter, made his heart thump once, hard.

"I'm so sorry, baby," she said to Olivia. He could hear the pain in her words.

Olivia must've, too, because she burrowed her head into Haley's shoulder.

Then Haley looked up at him, eyes baring her heart. She motioned him closer, but he hesitated. Could he weather Olivia's emotional storm?

Haley didn't give him a choice. She reached out and grabbed his shirtsleeve and gave him such a hard tug that he stumbled toward both girls. Being close, his only alternative was to put his arms around them.

Olivia turned her face toward him and pressed her cheek into his chest. He tightened his arm around her shoulders. Haley shifted, like she might be trying to back out of the embrace, but he tightened his arm around her, too.

She'd gotten him into this. She was staying.

It felt right, having her in this circle with him.

She looked up at him from entirely too close, and her cheeks were wet. "I miss her, too," Haley whispered.

And darn if he didn't find himself saying, voice rough, "Me, too."

And Olivia burst into tears. She clutched the back of his shirt in one hand.

He looked frantically at Haley, who gave a wet chuckle. She rested her hand on the crown of Olivia's head.

They stayed like that for several minutes, in a tight huddle. Until Olivia's sobs quieted to hiccups and he was sweating through his T-shirt from being so close to two other bodies in the hundred-plus degree Oklahoma sun.

Finally, Olivia pushed away, and he let them both go.

Olivia wiped her face with her fingers, and then Haley pressed a Kleenex she'd pulled from somewhere into his niece's hand.

"Thanks," Olivia said quietly. She didn't look up.

Haley looked at the top of Olivia's head. "I haven't been back here since the funeral."

Olivia's head came up. "You knew my mom?"

Haley glanced at Maddox, then back to the girl.

"Yeah. I did. I moved to Redbud Trails halfway through my senior year of high school. We were friends until she died."

Olivia's face lit up. Haley gestured to the dry, sun-baked grass. "You wanna sit for a little bit?"

Maddox made a noise, mostly to discourage her because of her dressy suit pants, but she dragged Olivia down with her and didn't seem worried about her slacks getting grass stains.

He sat with them, folding his too-long legs beneath him to complete their triangle.

"You're a lot like her," Haley said.

"Really?" Olivia's voice cracked, a sound between hope and uncertainty.

His heart ached with some of that uncertainty. Katie had been an inferno, bright and sometimes painful, burning out too quickly. *How much* was Olivia like her mother?

"Your eyes, your hair, your nose," Haley said. "The first day I saw you, I thought you looked just like her."

He nodded, listening. But not as raptly as Olivia was, with her face turned toward Haley, her eyes glued to her.

"Everyone liked Katie," Haley went on. "Wherever she went, people greeted her by name."

That was true, too.

"On my first day of school, I didn't know a soul. Before my first class was over, Katie had grabbed me and toted me with her down the hall and to our next class. She was so nice... and she didn't take *no* for an answer."

Maddox smiled. "She never did."

Olivia's head swiveled to him, her eyes serious, hopeful...

And he couldn't deny her.

Especially when Haley kicked the toe of his boot.

"She was a prankster. She would put bugs and lizards—one time even a snake—in our boots in the mudroom. Justin and I learned to check them every time."

Olivia giggled. He and his brother had never learned to laugh at her jokes. They'd always complained loudly to their mom.

He leaned back, letting his wrist take his weight. Some of the painful pressure in his chest was deflating, like a slow helium leak from a balloon.

"She was great at math and science, like you, Olivia," Haley remembered. She leaned back on her arm as well, her fingers overlapping Maddox's on the ground. Had she done that on purpose?

"And she was a planner, too," Haley continued. "She worked for weeks on what we were going to wear to prom, where we would eat supper, who we were going with..." She trailed off, a beautiful pink flush spreading across her face.

She must've realized exactly who she was talking to.

Maddox found himself grinning. She was finally getting a taste of her own medicine—the discomfort he'd felt ever since she'd burst into his life in vibrant color.

"She was a good friend." Haley sniffed, and he realized she was blinking back tears.

Olivia sniffled as well.

"And she loved you, kiddo," he said, through a sandpaper throat. "In the hospital with you, those first few days... she barely let anyone else hold you. She didn't want to let you go, even for a minute."

Olivia was crying again, silent tears streaming down her face, looking at him like...like she almost didn't believe him. "Why did she have to die?" she whispered.

He gathered her up, more natural about it this time. He shook his head, held her tightly. "I don't know, kiddo, I don't know."

Haley was wiping her eyes as unobtrusively as she could, but she was staying, sticking by his side, even though she probably needed to get back to her aunt.

But she was still here. When it hurt.

She placed a hand on Olivia's back, offering comfort.

Because Olivia needed her.

And then she reached out and touched his upper arm. Offering the same.

Because...he needed her.

Their eyes met and held. His insides churned like he'd ridden a whirly carnival ride. She did that to him. Discombobulated him until he wasn't sure which way was up.

But she also comforted him in a way no one else could.

She touched him, when no one else did.

He couldn't be...falling for her. Again. Could he?

He bent his head down over Olivia, the brim of his hat breaking the fragile connection of their gaze.

His heart was thundering now, he was sweating more than the baking sun really called for.

He wasn't falling for her. He couldn't be. She was just Katie's old friend. Now Olivia's friend. She'd helped him comfort Olivia, and he was grateful. That was all.

Right?

CHAPTER 5

"*A*re you going out to the Michaels' place today?"

Several days after the emotional scene at the cemetery, Haley settled in the floral-covered chair next to her aunt's bedside. The lunch she'd brought on a tray earlier lay on the bedside table, mostly untouched. She would take it back to the kitchen in a minute, but as long as Aunt Matilda was awake, she would sit and talk for a bit.

"I don't know."

Haley couldn't get Maddox off her mind. He and Livy were making strides from where they'd been at the beginning of the summer, when she'd come back into their lives.

He'd been calling the little girl every night from the road on the harvest crew.

And the last two nights, he'd called Haley. They'd talked for close to an hour each time, about her job as a marketing assistant for a big firm in Oklahoma City. About Justin and the accident and his recovery. About Livy.

But Maddox held back about himself.

"Am I getting too involved?" she asked her aunt. It was somewhat of a rhetorical question. "I started the summer wanting to help Livy with her ice cream business and maybe show her uncle what he was missing out on..."

"And now you've met the real man."

And she was afraid she was falling in love with him.

"I'm glad," Aunt Matilda smiled and patted Haley's hand. "I was afraid you were going to be hung up on that awful Patrick forever."

"Paul," Haley corrected gently. "And I've been over Paul for a while."

After spending time with Maddox this summer, she wondered if what she'd felt for the other man had been real love. In the beginning, she'd been infatuated with him. But as their relationship wore on, sometimes the things he said made her feel uncomfortable. He didn't think she was outgoing enough. Always wanted to go to more parties, when Haley would be perfectly content to stay home for a quiet dinner. They'd been together for two years and she'd been expecting a proposal. Instead, he'd left her behind for an out-of-state job. She'd *thought* she'd been heartbroken.

But if she'd loved him, why didn't she go with him? He hadn't asked, but what had stopped her from suggesting it?

She didn't know the answer to that question.

And she didn't know what to do about Maddox.

"Open your heart," Aunt Matilda said. "Don't be afraid to fall in love again. Life's too short to miss your second chances."

Coming from her aunt, the words were a bitter-sweet reminder.

The doorbell rang.

"Expecting someone?" her aunt asked.

"No."

When she pulled open the front door, there were Maddox and an effervescent Livy on the front stoop.

"What are you doing here?"

Livy's answer was a hug that Haley gratefully accepted. A step behind, Maddox held up a hand-packed quart of ice cream in each hand.

"New flavor, and we thought we'd better check on you and Mrs. Matilda."

It was thoughtful...and unexpected.

"Can I take it in to Aunt Matilda?" Livy asked,

bouncing on her toes. Bubbling with energy, as usual.

Haley agreed. "Grab a spoon from the kitchen," she called after the girl.

Maddox relinquished the carton to her and trailed her into the kitchen. They passed Livy on her way to Matilda's room.

Haley fished a pair of spoons out of the silverware drawer and offered one to Maddox.

"I shouldn't," he said, but he took the spoon anyway. "I had a taste at home already." He patted his stomach, and she rolled her eyes.

"It would take more than a taste to fatten you up. You work too hard."

A shadow flickered in his eyes, but he only smiled.

"So what flavor do we have here?" Haley dipped her spoon in what looked like a swirl of vanilla and caramel, but was... "Pumpkin bread?" she asked in surprise after the first bite.

"Yes, and it's addictive."

She sighed as she swallowed a few good bites. "This was just what I needed today." Both the ice cream and the visit.

"Glad we could oblige." His voice was a rumble of laughter, and Livy's giggle from the bedroom was an echo of the same.

He set the spoon down in the stainless steel sink. "Do you want to come to a rodeo this weekend? Like a... date?"

The tips of his ears had turned that endearing red.

"I thought you were on the road again."

"The kid I'm splitting shifts with needed to switch our days. I'll get back out there next week. Plus, I wanted to spend a little more time with Livy. School will start soon."

Their eyes met, and she read his sincerity. He was really trying with Livy.

He'd even changed his schedule.

Maybe he was figuring out that you never got back that lost time.

And she realized she didn't want to lose any time, either. No matter the risk.

She agreed in a whisper. "All right."

CHAPTER 6

wo days later, the realization that Matilda didn't have much time left finally became real for Haley.

She curled in a ball on the living room sofa and cuddled beneath one of Aunt Matilda's afghans, idly flipping through a photo album. She had rarely seen her aunt during her childhood, with her father moving the two of them around often. Until her senior year of high school, when Aunt Matilda had asked her to stay. They'd become close, almost as close as the mother she'd missed for years. Even when Haley had gone to college and made her life in Oklahoma City, they'd kept in touch with frequent phone calls and Matilda's visits to the city.

Unlike Haley's father, who had grown more and more distant. She might talk to him once every three months. At Christmas. Aunt Matilda had become the parent Haley needed.

What was Haley going to do without her? She still thought of Aunt Matilda's house as *home*, even after a decade away.

It was after nine when the soft knock came. At first she thought she'd imagined it.

But when it came a second time, she knew that whoever was out there wasn't going away. She peeked out the peephole to see Maddox's strong features and opened the door without thinking. It was when he blinked, visibly surprised, that she remembered she was wearing her painting sweatpants and rattiest T-shirt, she hadn't had a shower, her hair was tucked in a messy ponytail, and she probably had bags under her eyes.

It had been that kind of day.

His eyes softened when he saw her.

She tried to smile, but the weight of the day filled her eyes with tears.

She raised a hand to cover her face or ward him off—she hadn't completely made up her mind which —but he took her elbow in one of his big hands and tugged her forward.

He wrapped her in his muscled arms, and she sank into his embrace. She let him take her weight, buried her face in his chest, and breathed in leather and horse and cowboy.

"Bad day, huh?"

His words were a rumble under her cheek and hot in her hair and she hung on tightly.

She nodded, the top of her head bumping his chin.

"She's hanging in there?"

She nodded again. "Getting weaker," she said against the collar of his T-shirt.

"Still doesn't want to go to the hospital?"

This time she shook her head. Tears burned her eyes. The end was nearing for her aunt, but Haley wasn't ready to let her go.

He held her, giving her his strength. She knew she couldn't have him, not really. He was firmly anchored here in Redbud Trails, and she was eventually going back to her life in Oklahoma City. But she could have tonight.

When she'd settled a little, his hands moved to her waist, clasping her loosely.

She let go of him and raised both hands to wipe her cheeks.

Then he tipped her chin up, used the pad of his thumb to catch the tears she'd missed.

As she looked at those infinite brown eyes, shadowed in the darkness, he slid his palm against her

KISSED BY A COWBOY

jaw and leaned in.

And kissed her.


MINUTES LATER—MADDOX couldn't tell you how many—they sat together on the porch swing. He'd given Haley the quart of ice cream Olivia had sent, and she'd brought out two spoons, but he'd barely tasted the half-melted sweet. He wanted to remember the taste of Haley, not ice cream.

"How'd you know I needed this tonight?" she asked. Her head lolled on his shoulder, and his arm rested around her.

They fit perfectly together.

Just like at her senior prom.

Except for the fact that she was leaving, and he was stuck here in Redbud Trails, trying to save the family farm, trying to keep his brother afloat, trying to be a father to Olivia.

"Olivia saw me heading out the door and wanted you to try it. Sorry if it's melted."

"I'm not." The smile in her voice made him smile, too, and he squeezed her shoulders.

"What's she calling it?"

He wanted to ask her about her aunt again, but he knew how sometimes when you were so deep in something, you just needed to think and talk about the silly little things in life.

So that's what he gave her.

"She said 'peach cobbler.'"

"Mmm. I like it. I predict it will be popular."

He shook his head. "You'd predict that about any of her creations."

"I would not. Not the bad ones."

Haley's early predictions about the business had been right. Things were taking off. Orders kept coming in, and Olivia spent hours running her machine. She was talking about maybe needing a second deep freezer. And she was thrilled about it.

Finally finished, Haley set the quart on the floor near their feet, and when she straightened, she turned so they were almost face-to-face and laid her palms on his cheeks.

He jumped from the cold.

She giggled. "Sorry."

But she wasn't really. He took her cold hands in his and rubbed them, providing friction, and he hoped, warmth. He was certainly warm enough for the both of them.

"Can I ask you something?"

"Yeah."

"How come you've never talked about Katie? With Livy, I mean."

He breathed in deep. "After she died, Livy was so little. Mom couldn't bear to talk about her. Those first months were hard on all of us. Then mom had her stroke and just gave up, and Justin and I didn't talk about anything. We were focused on surviving.

"I guess I never realized Livy needed it. Not until you came along. Now she wants to hear about Katie all the time."

She smiled against his shoulder.

"Has Justin picked out any classes for the fall?"

"Yeah. But he still has to go to the school and register."

Maddox wasn't ready to believe that his brother would do it. But Justin was at least talking about getting back to having a life instead of moping around in that recliner all day.

It was an improvement, if a small one. Haley had made her mark there, too.

The tip of his boot dragged on the porch floor. Their swing barely moved. She didn't seem to mind.

"Don't forget about our date Saturday. Do you still think you'll be able to come?"

"Unless Aunt Matilda gets much worse. She's looking forward to hearing all about it."

"Good."

He tucked her close again and rested his chin on top of her head. He liked being with her like this. He could imagine spending all their summer nights together, talking about their days and just *being together*.

He wanted it. Wanted it so bad he could taste it.

And that was just plain dangerous.

But it didn't stop him.


HALEY WAS wide-awake when Maddox left a half hour later. She needed sleep, but instead of climbing into bed, she stared out the window where his taillights had disappeared.

She was in love with him.

Forget about a teenager's crush on her friend's handsome older brother.

She'd seen the real man. Someone who worked his butt off to take care of his family. Someone who held her, not asking for anything. Giving comfort.

Someone real.

Not the dream she'd imagined for so long.

How was she going to go back to her old life after this was all over?

# CHAPTER 7

*S*aturday came, right on the heels of a new pile of medical bills. Maddox had thought they'd gotten through all of them, but a phone call to their insurance company revealed the truth—here was another stack waiting to be paid.

He'd gotten complacent these last few days, talking with Haley on the phone. Kissing her.

Thinking that they might have some kind of future together.

What had he been thinking?

He had a kid, a brother, and a farm to take care of, and bills out the wazoo.

Later that night, when Haley joined him and Justin and Livy at the rodeo arena one town over, those thoughts kept him company. He couldn't get past them enough to make polite conversation.

She noticed. Of course.

Sitting next to him on the crowded bleachers, she bumped his knee with hers, smiling sideways at him. Livy was on her other side, and Justin took up another seat past her. Maddox had been shocked when his brother had asked to ride along. He hadn't wanted to get off the farm at all, and now he wanted to attend a rodeo?

But Maddox had helped him load his crutches into the truck without a word.

"Did you ever want to do rodeo as a child?" Haley asked.

"For a few weeks," he admitted. He squinted down at the action in the fenced-off, dirt-packed arena. A bell rang and a horse took off from the starting gate at one side, its rider clinging to the reins and urging it on as it raced around three barrels in a triangle, then back out the gate where it had started.

"What happened?" Haley asked after the barrel rider had finished her loop.

"Took a ride on a sheep. Fell off, and decided football was safer."

"That's my brilliant brother," Justin put in from Livy's other side.

Maddox let Justin take the conversational reins,

talking about their childhood and Katie riding barrels.

Until Haley bumped him again. "Wanna take a walk? I'll buy you a pretzel."

He considered her. She was wearing a cute pair of jeans, boots, and a black Stetson he'd never seen before. It made her look right at home in this crowd. "This is my date. I'm buying."

She met his gaze squarely. "I'm glad you remembered," she teased softly.

She was right. He'd let his worry about the medical bills take over his thoughts.

But it was also his life. He had to support his family. He refused to do what his dad had done and give up.

She followed him down the bleachers, and when he started off to the food trucks, she slid easily under his arm. Her boots put the top of her head level with his chin, and she felt *right* there. Again.

One of Justin's friends called out to Maddox, and he waved, a flop of his hand on her shoulder.

"Wanna tell me what's wrong?" They stood in line behind a few people with the same idea about the pretzels, and she looked up at him with slightly raised brows, waiting for an answer.

"Nothing for you to worry about," he said. "You've

got enough going on with your aunt." And being broke wasn't exactly something he wanted to own up to. He had a little pride.

"That's true." Her chin lifted toward him. "But I can still listen."

He shook his head slightly. Not tonight. His problems were still too raw.

She looked off into the distance. "Once I get back to Oklahoma City, maybe you could drive down for a visit..."

Haley continued to speak, but he heard very little. He'd known she would be leaving, knew this was only temporary, but how could she speak of it so casually? Her words, the very thought of her leaving, felt like a punch in the gut.

IT HAD TAKEN Haley so long to build up the courage to ask him to visit her in the city, and then...nothing. No answer. No response whatsoever.

She'd thought...

She'd hoped his kisses meant something. That his arm around her shoulder, the way he'd comforted her the other night, meant his feelings were growing. Growing to match what hers already were.

And here they were, on a date. A date he'd

requested. Not a *let's go as friends* thing, but a real, honest-to-goodness date. And yet...

Had she been kidding herself?

Was he just enjoying a summer romance? Was he being a courteous cowboy, or simply returning her kindness to Livy?

They inched forward in the pretzel line. She took a deep breath, steeling her courage, and looked up at him. He met her gaze, his eyes dark beneath the brim of his hat. He didn't smile, but the corners of his eyes crinkled.

And she knew.

He cared about her.

But something held him back.

The gal behind the counter cleared her throat, and Maddox placed their order. He bought her a paper-wrapped pretzel and a bottle of water and led her away from the crowded line.

"So that's a *no*?" she asked tentatively.

He shook his head slightly. What did that mean? Was it *no*, that his non-response hadn't meant *no*, or just *no* to her question in general?

He led them clear of the crowd, stopped, and faced her. "I'm going to have to pick up some extra work," he said. "I doubt I'll have time to come down, even if it's for a weekend."

Oh. After what he'd said the other night, she'd thought he might be cutting back on extra work.

"Livy needs you," she said in a small voice.

"She also needs new school clothes and a roof over her head," he muttered.

They meandered toward the stands, not in any hurry, finally stopping behind them, in the small patch of shadow. On the other side of the bleachers, the arena lights lit everything, but here it was dark.

"Justin said you might have a lead on a job with Livy's school. Coaching football and teaching a little."

"So y'all have been talking about me?"

"He mentioned it."

Maddox blew out a breath. She couldn't tell if he was frustrated that she'd been in his business or frustrated about the job. "I can't take that job," he said, the anger evident, though she didn't understand it.

"Why not?" She was angry, too, though not for herself. She was trying not to feel anything for herself—the last few minutes had shattered her hopes for anything with him. But Livy needed him. "You'd have more time for Livy, all summer off—"

"I'd still have a farm to manage, but that's not the point. I can't take that job."

"If it's about being on the sidelines—"

"It's not," he said, and his voice rang with hurt.

"About expectations?"

He laughed, a harsh sound.

"You want the truth?" he asked roughly.

The words hit her like a strong gust of wind. She felt like she was on her toes, almost lifting off her feet.

She reached out and touched his arm. "Maddox..."

He didn't turn toward her. He just stared into the shadows beneath the bleachers.

Twilight had gone and darkness had fallen. She could barely see him in the dim light that seeped from the arena.

"The truth is, everyone around here thinks I finished my degree, but I'm a year short. The only reason the principal offered me that job is he thinks I've got a piece of paper with my name on it. But I don't."

She knew about a man's pride. Her own father had chased jobs across the nation, wanting to *provide* for his girl. She could only imagine how having to admit something like this was hitting Maddox.

"Without a college education, jobs like working on the harvest crew are all I've got. With Justin out of commission and medical bills piling up...if the price of cattle falls any more, we'll be butchering our

LACY WILLIAMS

own. Working is all I know how to do. It's all I'm good for."

She grabbed his arm and yanked until he rounded on her.

She looked up at him with all the love swelling in her heart and into her throat, making it impossible to speak. She swallowed and forced the words out.

"No, it's not," she whispered. "No, it's *not*."

She slid her hands behind his neck and tugged him down toward her.

He seemed to understand. His lips slanted over hers, his hands slipped around her waist, and if he held her just a little too tightly, well, that was okay with her.

A loudspeaker squealed, breaking the moment. She backed away a step, touched her lips with a trembling hand. A disembodied voice announced the start of the bull riding.

Looking down, she saw both of their hats had fallen into the dust.

She bent to pick them up and offered his to him. He took it, but she didn't let go. Their eyes met and connected over the top.

"I don't know what's gonna happen," he said in a low voice.

Neither did she. She didn't know how long Aunt

Matilda would hold on, or how Livy's ice cream business would do.

Or if she'd walk away at the end of all of this with her heart intact.

But she couldn't walk away from Maddox right now.

She entwined her fingers with his and tugged him back up into the stands.

# CHAPTER 8

*I*t was over.

Aunt Matilda was gone.

Haley sat through the funeral on the first pew in the little country church. Numb.

She and her aunt had made most of the arrangements in advance, so there had only been a few things to take care of, although she'd spent the last two days in a sea of paperwork, insurance claims, and lawyers.

How could it be that Haley would never see Aunt Matilda again? That her closest family member was lost to her?

Tears spilled over again, and Haley bowed her head, covered her face with her hands, and let them come.

She missed her. If only she'd made more time to come home since she'd left for college.

She'd always thought *there's time*.

And now, there was no time left.

A warm, wide hand rested on the center of her back. Maddox.

They were seated so close, she could feel the heat of his thigh next to hers. He'd been a steady presence the last couple of days. Bringing her food when she'd forgotten to eat. Answering the door to the church ladies when Haley couldn't face their kindness for her grief. He'd answered his phone in the wee hours when she couldn't sleep.

Olivia and Justin had been in and out, tiptoeing around and whispering like she was fine china. But this wasn't going to break her.

If she'd learned anything this summer, it was that cowgirls got back up after they got bucked off. And they didn't let go of what was important.

She was in love with Maddox.

She hadn't figured out how she was going to make it work between them. She had a job, back in Oklahoma City. Her boss had granted her another few days of leave to wrap things up, but he expected her back soon.

And Maddox was very firmly entrenched in Redbud Trails. He wasn't letting go of the farm without a fight. And he shouldn't. It was their family legacy, the place where Katie had grown up and Olivia could connect with her mother.

Everything was a muddle.

But today, all Haley could do was grieve. With Maddox beside her, holding her up, she could let Aunt Matilda go.

She would wait for a chance to talk to Maddox later.


A WEEK LATER, Haley was still waiting.

Maddox had had to leave for the harvest crew the day after the funeral. The four-day separation had distanced them. He'd come home quieter, more reserved. She didn't know how to get their closeness back.

This morning, he'd come to help her load her car. It hadn't taken long, and now as he stowed the last of her boxes in the trunk, she stood in the empty dining room.

Out the window, a *For Sale* sign out front was the tangible sign that nothing would ever be the same.

She hesitated inside the front door, looking at Maddox's broad shoulders as he waited by her car.

What if... what if she'd been wrong about his feelings? For several days, she'd been mired in grief. All the insurance paperwork had kept her busy, slightly on edge, and frustrated.

And now Maddox was back, and that insidious voice in her head—a voice that sounded remarkably like Paul's—kept reminding her that she *wasn't enough*. She had never been enough to keep her father from chasing the next best job. Paul had found her wanting—criticizing her because she wasn't outgoing enough, telling her she needed to be a perfect hostess when they eventually got married.

What if...what if Maddox found her wanting as well?

Steeling herself with a deep breath, she stepped outside her aunt's door, trying not to think about how it was the last time she would, and locked it behind her.

His hands rested casually in his front pockets. His Stetson threw a shadow over his eyes, and she couldn't read them. His body language was casual, friendly.

But not welcoming.

She stopped several feet away, keys jangling in her nerveless fingers.

"Well, that's it," she said on an exhale.

If he would just give her an indication that he felt the same way he had when he'd kissed her before, at the rodeo...

But he only nodded, unsmiling.

"I'm not ready," she said softly. "To say goodbye."
To the house, to her aunt's memory.

But especially to him.

MADDOX FISTED his hands in his jeans pockets, the muscles in his arms aching from wanting to reach for her.

He kept his jaw clenched to hold back the tide. Words like, *please don't leave me*. Words like, *I love you*.

She deserved better than a cowboy who was fighting for every paycheck.

His dad had given up, failed the family, nearly lost the farm.

But Maddox refused to do the same. Even if he was one overdue mortgage payment away from losing the place, he couldn't give up.

And that meant a lot of hard work.

How could he commit to—how could he ask Haley to commit to—a long-distance relationship when he knew he couldn't commit to it himself? He couldn't. His focus had to be on keeping his family afloat.

He'd watched his mother get beaten down by life

and a husband who'd ultimately failed the family. He couldn't ask Haley to do the same.

Or worse, start a relationship with her and a year down the road, have her decide to ditch the loser who was still working his butt off for a chunk of land.

He'd die if she walked away from him. He felt about like he was dying now. Like a big ol' bull had stepped on his chest cavity.

The best he could hope for was in a few months to have made some good money, put another nest egg aside, and when he'd proved he could support his family, call her. With any luck, she wouldn't fall in love with someone else.

All those words settled in his heart, tucked away. "Drive safe." He didn't add, *call me when you get there* or *I'll miss you.*

He couldn't bear the uncertainty in her eyes, so he turned away, yanking open her car door. She slipped under his arm, silent. Watchful. Waiting.

But he couldn't give her what she needed, so he said nothing.

And she started the car and drove away.

## CHAPTER 9

"*H*ello?"

"Is this Maddox Michaels?"

"Speaking. Who's this?"

"Dan Crane."

Hearing the junior high principal's voice on the phone pulled Maddox up short. He was on a three-day weekend back from the harvest crew, driving to town to make Olivia's weekly ice cream delivery to the restaurant that acted as a consignment agent for her, but now he stopped his truck on the side of the state highway.

"Dan. I've been meaning to return your calls."

He took a deep breath and decided to come clean.

"Actually, I haven't," he said. "Been meaning to call."

"Look, Maddox, we need you. There's no one else around qualified to coach—"

"I'm not qualified to teach," he said. And that shut the other man up. "I never finished my degree. I was a year short. I let everybody around here think I was done because I was too chicken to admit I was so much like my father."

His free hand clenched the bottom of the steering wheel.

There was a beat of silence before Dan spoke. "I wish I'd known this sooner."

Yeah. No kidding.

More silence and Maddox wanted to get out of the uncomfortable conversation. "I'll let you go—"

"Hang on a minute, Michaels. I'm thinking. You know, if we can get you enrolled..."

"What?"

While Maddox listened in shock, the other man outlined a plan for Maddox to finish his degree and get certified to teach—by Christmastime.

He wasn't even sure what he'd agreed to by the time the call ended twenty minutes later, but he did know that in one phone conversation, hope had come back to him.

But having a job didn't make up for losing Haley.

Every time he breathed in deeply, it felt like

knives slicing through his lungs. He missed her so much.

It had been almost three weeks, and he'd heard nothing. Not that he'd expected to—he'd made his wishes clear that last day. But now, he was dying inside, a little each day.

He was still mulling the new job offer over when he got home with the boxed meal the restaurant manager had pushed on him.

Only to find Justin on his feet, wrestling with the old brown recliner.

"What're you doing?" Maddox dumped the food on the kitchen table and rushed to take the weight of the chair. Last thing Justin needed was for that chair to topple over and land on his only remaining good leg.

"I got to thinking," Justin said, huffing. "That it's time to get rid of this old thing."

Their eyes met over the top of the stinky chair.

He knew what Justin was saying. More than the recliner, it was time to let the past go.

His dad had sat in the chair and drunk himself to death. Maddox barely had any good memories of the man.

Ma had sat in this chair, swallowed by her grief. After she'd lost Katie, she'd lost herself.

Justin had almost done the same. His injury had made him give up on life.

But if he was man enough to get out of the chair, he was on the road to total recovery. His hip might not be fully functional, and he might always have a limp, but he could move on.

Maddox felt a hot burn behind his eyes. He cleared his throat. "I'm proud of you."

"Yeah, yeah." Justin leaned down to pick up the crutch he'd laid across the fireplace hearth. "After you take that out to the dump, you need to get in your truck and head to Oklahoma City."

Maddox grunted. He angled the chair toward the door, eyeing the frame. The chair wasn't going to fit upright.

"I'm not kidding," Justin said. "You can't just let a girl like Haley get away."

Maddox pushed the chair across the floor. It hung up on a patch of old carpet and he almost fell over the top of it, getting a good wallop in the stomach when it rebounded.

"Mad. I'm serious."

"She's the one who left," he huffed. She'd left him behind. Again.

"And you've been moping around here for three weeks. You've got two feet and a truck. So go get her and bring her back."

His heart panged once, hard. "It's not that easy. I've got a lead on a job, but I've got to prove myself—"

"Prove what?" Justin demanded. "Prove that you're just as much of an idiot as our father? She's in love with you—if you haven't messed that up. She'll stand by you."

He wanted to believe...wanted to believe it so badly.

Maddox's heart thudded in his chest. "I've been pretty stupid."

"No kidding. What else is new? But she fell in love with you knowing that football players have a couple screws loose, so this little act of stupidity probably hasn't surprised her much."

Could he really take Justin's advice?

What if she couldn't forgive him for breaking her heart?

Worse than that, what if he never tried to put it back together?

HALEY HAD SETTLED into her normal routine.

Sort of.

She went to work. And stared at her computer screen all day. She wasn't getting a lot done.

She came home. And tried not to stare at her phone, willing Maddox to call.

She'd called his house and spoken to Livy several times, checking on the business, checking on the girl.

She'd shied away from asking about Maddox. When Livy had offered tidbits like *he liked the root beer float flavor*, Haley had *mm-hmmed* and moved on.

What was wrong with her?

She had a car. Gas. Keys. She could drive back to Redbud Trails any time. She wanted to take the man by the shoulders and shake him. Or maybe kiss him.

She didn't know what she'd been thinking that last day. Maybe she'd let her grief blind her, or her fear.

She *knew* there was something between her and Maddox. It had been too strong to deny, and too strong to fade away.

She'd talked herself into a weekend trip and had her keys dangling from her fingers when she exited her front door. And stopped short.

There was a big, dusty truck in her driveway.

She barely registered the truck before a tall, dusty cowboy stood in her way, too.

She threw herself at him. And he caught her.

"What took you so long?" she mumbled into his shoulder.

He rumbled a laugh. "Sorry." She felt the press of his chin in her hair. "It took this big, dumb *Ox* a little bit to get things figured out."

She tilted her chin back and squinted up at him. "Don't call yourself dumb."

He used the opportunity to rub his thumb along the line of her jaw.

"So what did you figure out?" she whispered.

"Well, the financial situation is still a little sticky," he said. "But mostly, I realized that I was focusing on the wrong things, like your dad did."

He brushed a kiss across her temple.

"And letting the best thing in my life get away, kind of like my dad did."

Now he brushed a kiss across her cheek.

"And I don't want to be like either of them."

"You're not—" she started to say.

And he sure kissed her like he agreed.

When they broke away minutes later, both panting and out-of-breath, he noticed the keys dangling from her hand. "Going somewhere?"

"I was on my way to Redbud Trails." She couldn't help the shy smile. "You're not the only one who was being less-smart than they should be." She looked down briefly but then back up at him, his over-whelming presence—and his kisses—giving her courage. "I shouldn't have left without telling you I was in love with you."

He lit up from the inside out.

"And not because of your bank account," she went on. "Or your farm."

He lifted his eyebrows.

"It's definitely because of your niece's ice cream." She stood on her tiptoes and brushed a kiss against his lips. "I want a piece of the business."

He leaned down and kissed her beneath her jaw. "You already own a piece of it."

"Hmm." She giggled and tucked her chin down when his hot breath tickled her neck. "I guess it must be something else, then."

She pushed on his shoulders until he was far enough away that she could see his face. "It's because of who you are. The man who wouldn't give up on his brother. Who redid the kitchen to make a little girl's dream come true."

The quiet joy on his face made the heartfelt confession easy.

"Wanna know why I'm in love with you?" he asked.

Her heart soared up into her throat, and she nodded.

He cupped her jaw in one hand. "Same reason. Because of who you are. Your quiet spirit and gentle heart that saw my niece's needs and found a way to meet them. You reached out to Justin when the rest of the outside world forgot him and gave him the courage to go on." He swallowed hard. "And you found a way inside my heart when I thought it was too full of worrying about everything else." His expression darkened. "I don't know how everything's going to work out."

"That's okay. We can figure it out together."

"Together." He breathed in deeply. "That sounds so right."

And he kissed her again.

THE END

# EPILOGUE

## ONE MONTH LATER

*M*addox threw his pickup into Park and crossed his wrists over the steering wheel, leaning slightly forward. Even though it was only mid-morning, the intense August heat meant he was blasting the A/C, and it hit him full in the face as he looked up at the imposing brick façade of the administration building at the small college.

He squinted against the morning sunlight; every time he blinked, grit from lack of sleep scraped his eyes. He'd left South Dakota after dark last night, putting in as many hours on the combine as he could before coming home. He hated leaving the custom harvest before the season was completely over, but Dan had trusted him with the teaching and coaching job, even though he didn't deserve it yet, and he couldn't mess this up.

He was wiped, but he made himself push open the truck door and stand. He'd stopped a couple hours ago when he'd found himself nodding off behind the wheel, shored himself up on coffee and a greasy breakfast burrito.

Now he was a little afraid he smelled like stale fast food. And his muscles protested the hours of inactivity. The college was a forty-five minute drive from Redbud Trails, but he was almost home. He just had to get through the enrollment process.

He needed to check in on Livy and Justin. He'd spoken briefly to Haley on the phone late last night.

It was busier than he'd thought it would be the last day of summer break—classes started on Monday. Kids streamed past him as he hesitated on the threshold. Then he stood in the atrium, looking up at the skylight. He could remember his first day at OU in Norman—a campus that made this one look puny. He'd been on top of the world his junior year—with two years still to play and riding a football scholarship. Things were sure different now, coming back after a decade away.

A kid brushed past, his backpack knocking into

Maddox's shoulder and breaking him from his brief reverie. That kid looked young. They all did. Wearing clothes he didn't get, with wires hanging out of their ears. Messenger bags.

Man, he felt old.

Another kid manned the desk at the advisement office. He popped his gum as he looked over the Associate's degree Dan had helped him scrape together from his old transcripts, checking off boxes on another sheet of paper before handing Maddox a list of the classes required if he wanted to get his bachelor's degree next May.

Then he found himself punted back to the atrium, kids streaming past him in both directions as he read the list.

Nearly twenty-two hours between two semesters, and that on top of teaching and coaching.

Could he even do this?

MID-MORNING, Haley was chopping walnuts in the Michaels's kitchen when the back door opened and Maddox strode inside.

The sunlight streaming in the windows behind him silhouetted the droop of his shoulders. Lines around his mouth showed his exhaustion. He set a packet of papers on the island, even that movement speaking weariness.

"Hey," she greeted him.

His eyes showed his surprise, but the only response she got was a scorching press of his mouth against hers, and then he disappeared up the stairs and presumably to his bedroom.

She stood there dumbly for a minute, staring after him. Since they'd declared their feelings to each other over a month ago, they'd had to content themselves with extended phone conversations and one long weekend visit as he'd worked to finish out the season with the harvest crew.

She'd thought things were going well—as well as they could be. But his behavior just now sent a shiver of uncertainty through her.

She couldn't resist. She tiptoed up the stairs and down the hall and tapped on Maddox's bedroom door. No answer.

She'd never been in his bedroom. She turned the knob—unlocked—and peeked inside. Maddox was facedown on the bed, his face turned to the opposite wall.

Either he was asleep or he didn't want to be disturbed. She slipped away, closing the door quietly, and returned to the kitchen and her walnuts.

She was still reeling from his non-response when

Livy rushed into the kitchen, going a hundred miles an hour, as usual.

"Was that uncle M?"

"Yeah." Haley forced a smile for the girl's sake. "Looks like he made it home safely."

But her stomach remained knotted. Or maybe it was the knowledge that she was about to make a change that couldn't be undone.

She used the knife and her hand to transport the chopped walnuts to a small resealable container.

Livy snapped on the lid. "I'm ready to go if you are."

She wasn't. Not really.

Justin meandered in from the living room, mashing his hat on his head. "Heading out?" He did a double take, and Haley realized she must not be hiding her emotions as well as she'd thought. "You okay?"

She shored up her smile. "I'll be all right."

Livy's hand slipped into hers. The girl had such a tender heart, just like her mama.

Eventually, they'd head to Weatherford, but for now she and Livy stopped at Aunt Matilda's house.

She stood rooted in the grass, staring for long moments at the realtor's sign that now had a bold *Sold* attached to the top.

Finally she shook herself from the funk and followed Livy inside.

Livy, seeming older than her years, wandered through each empty room with her arms outstretched.

Haley followed slower, her fingers dragging on the windowsill in what had once been her bedroom. Touching the wall in Matilda's bedroom. Spinning a slow circle in the kitchen.

Her grief still surprised her at unexpected times, prompting tears at work one morning and forcing her to excuse herself from a girls' night when her friends had chosen Matilda's favorite romantic comedy.

And today was more painful than she'd imagined. Selling the house was giving up the last link to her aunt.

It was like saying goodbye all over again.

Livy had gone out to the car as Haley hesitated on the front porch.

From her pocket, her cell phone rang. She glanced at it. Her boss.

"Hi, Mr. Peters."

"You took a personal day?" her boss said in lieu of a greeting. He didn't sound happy.

She took a breath, still off-balance from her tour of Matilda's home. "Yes, I put it on the calendar over three weeks ago. I'm closing on my Aunt's... on my late Aunt's house today."

There was a pause, and then his voice came back in a lower register. "We have to present to Gallager on Monday."

"I turned in the graphics files yesterday—"

"Not with the revisions they requested. I emailed those to you last week."

"I didn't see any revisions." She couldn't have missed something this important, could she?

Unfortunately, she wasn't sure. Her heart was in Redbud Trails, and she often found herself counting the hours until the weekends, when she could come up and spend time with Maddox—or more often lately, with Livy.

"I have the email right here in my Sent Mail," her boss said, and he sounded positively steamed now.

"I'm sorry, but I don't remember seeing it." She glanced at her watch. "I have the closing in about an hour. I'm not sure how long it will take. I'll work from here this afternoon and see if I can get to the revisions you want."

It was the best she could do. Her boss was silent for a long time, and she squeezed her eyes shut, scrunching up all her facial muscles. He wasn't happy.

And she was right. "Six months ago, I would've

said you were my brightest up-and-coming employee. And now... You've got to get your head on straight, Carston. If you want to keep working here, stop wasting my time."

He hung up, and she found herself blinking back tears for a whole other reason. She pinched the bridge of her nose, not wanting to alarm Livy. The kid already had enough burdens, dealing with one uncle who was still battling out of depression and an older-than-her-years concern over Maddox's financial situation.

After the closing, she'd planned to take Livy shopping for school clothes, but either they would have to take an abbreviated trip or delay until another time.


AFTER A FEW HOURS OF SLEEP, Maddox forced himself to get up. There were things to do. He was expected to report to the junior high office first thing Monday morning, which meant he only had the weekend to catch up on all the household things he'd fallen behind on by being gone most of the summer.

And had he dreamed it, or had Haley been standing in his kitchen this morning? He'd been so wiped he'd only had one thought—*get to his bed*.

But now a fuzzy memory of her dear face intruded.

The house was quiet. A headache pounded relentlessly behind his eyes as he made a thick ham and cheese sandwich and ate it standing at the island counter.

Someone had left a pile of unopened mail on the nook table. He tried to ignore it, but the more he tried, the bigger the pile seemed to grow in his peripheral vision.

Finally, he gave in with a sigh. Opened the first one. Bill. Late notice. Bill. Oh, junk mail, that was a nice break.

He found himself rubbing aching muscles in his neck. He didn't have to look at his checkbook to know this month was going to be tight. He had his last harvest paycheck in his pocket, right next to the simple silver ring he'd bought three weeks ago, when he'd still been riding high on exchanging *I love yous* with Haley.

Haley.

He missed her viscerally. Wanted her here permanently—hence the ring—but what could he offer her? An empty house, while he was working and going to school? She'd basically be his nanny and take care of Livy.

Why in the heck would she accept a proposal

like that?

It was better to wait.

Because he knew that things were going to get a lot tougher before they got better.


"MAYBE if we wedge this larger spatula inside," Livy said.

Haley nodded. "We could rub down the spatula with something—butter maybe?—that wouldn't affect the taste of the ice creams but would lubricate it when you're ready to put the lid on..."

Livy's eyes lit up, and she turned to the fridge.

It was almost supper time. Haley was back in her usual happy place—the Michaels's kitchen.

She watched the girl shove the rubber spatula into the cardboard tube. She wanted to create a new product with two ice cream flavors, and they were struggling to package the concoction without having the two ice cream flavors overlap.

And it didn't help that Haley was distracted. They'd completely taken over one side of the kitchen and the island, while Maddox was set up at the nook table. He had a stack of college textbooks on one chair. What looked like a junior high schoolbook was spread on the table in front of him, along with a stapled stack of papers and a notebook. On the right side of the table was a pile of hastily organized envelopes she recognized as utilities bills.

He paused frequently, stopping to rub the back of his neck. Stressed out.

He'd been attentive but quiet as Livy had modeled three outfits for him after they'd returned from Weatherford. Haley had barricaded herself in Livy's bedroom, using the time to make the changes to the marketing campaign materials that her boss wanted. She'd emailed them to him, though she hadn't heard back yet. Now it was after business hours, and he was likely gone for the weekend. Monday morning might not be pleasant, but if he wasn't working over the weekend, why should she?

There'd been no real chance for Haley and Maddox to talk, because Livy had commandeered her to help with the ice cream before supper.

Now she held the bucket and spatula beneath the lip of the blast freezer as Livy turned the knob. They filled half of the container and then scooted to the counter where Livy had her smaller, personal ice cream maker also filled with a flavor. They added it to the empty side and then held their breaths as Haley gently extracted the spatula.

"We'd better get this in the freezer to keep the flavors from mixing," she told Livy.

Livy's eyes lit up as the spatula came out without

much resistance. It was covered in a thin layer of creamy goodness, and Haley raised it to her mouth to lick it.

The legs of Maddox's chair scraped the floor, and her eyes flicked up. He'd pushed his chair back from the table.

And he was staring at her mouth.

She pulled the tip of the spatula out with an audible *pop*. "You want a taste?"

She held out the spatula to him as she approached, but instead of taking it, he grabbed her wrist and pulled her down onto his lap.

"Mad—"

He cut her off with a searing kiss that had Haley forgetting everything else until Livy giggled.

"Hey!" Justin's voice rang out, breaking the moment as he banged in through the back door. He set two bulging plastic bags on the corner of the island and grabbed Livy, putting one hand over her eyes. "There are impressionable young people here. And Livy's in here, too!"

Livy giggled and shoved his hand off.

Maddox made no move to let her go, resting his chin against her temple, his arm a welcome weight at her waist.

Some of her uncertainty from earlier began to dissipate. He might be stressed out, she might be facing a difficult situation at work, but they were *together*.

Justin unpacked Styrofoam to-go containers from the bags, the greasy-good smell of fries and burgers wafting through the room. Her mouth watered.

"Why don't you put this aside for a little while?" Haley asked Maddox softly. "At least long enough to eat something."

She was close enough that she felt his sigh. He ran a hand through his hair but began piling up his things.

She squeezed his shoulder and pushed up to stand, moving to join Justin and Livy at the island. She popped open the nearest container and wrinkled her nose. Corned beef on rye. Maddox's.

"How'd the closing go?" Justin asked casually, his attention on unloading the condiments. "No last-minute issues?"

She stole a fry from Maddox's box of food, turning to take it to him, but he was frozen, half out of the chair.

"That was today?" He took the box from her, setting it on the table but ignoring the food. His eyes were locked on her face.

And her emotions from earlier bubbled back to the surface. It was easier to turn back and take her own box of food from Justin, who held it out to her. "Yeah. Livy and I stopped by Matilda's house to—say goodbye." She stumbled over the words, but got them out with only a small gasp.

She wobbled, and Livy was there, putting an arm around her waist.

She wiped at the single tear that wanted to fall. When she looked up, Justin and Maddox were having some kind of silent conversation with their eyes.

And then Maddox was there too, putting his arm around her opposite shoulder so she was sandwiched between uncle and niece.

Tears threatened again but she swallowed them back. "I miss her, but she's not there anymore. In the house."

Maddox squeezed her shoulders.

HOURS LATER, Maddox sat on the couch, the living room dark around him. He'd put away the syllabus, the junior high textbook, and the college textbooks after supper. He was sorely disappointed, frustrated in himself that he'd forgotten about Haley's big day.

She'd been emotional just thinking about it, almost in tears, and there was only so much comfort he could give her with a hug.

And there was a part of him that worried that now that her last tie to Redbud Trails was cut, she wouldn't be up here as much on the weekends.

He was already going to be pressed for time when the semester kicked off next week. Between teaching at the junior high and the football season—practices would start immediately—and then his own schooling... He didn't even know how they were going to see each other.

He'd managed to get two of this semester's classes in two separate all-weekend blitzes, but he would still have to carry a three-hour night class into December, then twelve hours during the spring semester.

He couldn't help but worry that Haley was going to get tired of him. Get tired of him constantly working, tire of the long days.

He could hear her voice from Livy's room, where they'd still been talking ice cream even as she helped Livy get ready for bed.

Even the stresses and worries weren't enough to keep him awake after his sleepless night on the road.

He found himself nodding off with his head lolled back against the couch.

Time passed. He told himself to get up.

Dozed on.

Felt her fingertips brush against his forehead and

sensed her leaning over him.

She brushed a kiss across his cheek.

"We need to talk."

That was the last thing he remembered.


WE NEED TO TALK.

Words to inspire fear in any man.

Maddox woke with a crick in his neck and his face in a pool of drool on the living room couch cushion. A beam of sunlight slanted through the blinds and hit him right in the eyes.

He sat up with a grunt, rubbing one hand over his face.

Had he imagined her words? A boulder in the depths of his gut told him otherwise.

The boulder remained through a quick shower and cup of coffee—which only made him nauseated. He did his best to ignore the pain as he headed out to the barn.

He met Justin coming as he was leaving. "The horses are fed and watered. I'm going to the feed store. Ryan's short-handed this week, and I've been picking up some hours there."

That his brother had been up and taken care of the animals was a little shock, but Justin's words jarred Maddox to a stop. "You got a job?"

"It's only a few hours, until he hires someone else. It's not much," Justin muttered, brushing past Maddox and taking the porch steps as fast as his injured hip would allow.

It wasn't much, but for Justin it was a giant leap. As far as Maddox knew, he hadn't done much of anything productive since he'd crashed off that bull over a year ago. Now he had a job. And was helping out around the farm, saving Maddox and Ryan the trouble.

Wonders never ceased.

"You should take a break this weekend," Justin called back to him. "The world won't fall down around you if you take a couple days off." The screen door slammed behind him.

*Days off?* What were those?

Maddox wheeled in a circle, stuck. Unsure what to do now that he didn't have chores. There was the barn that needed a coat of paint—that they couldn't afford—and the south field would need to be cleared if they were going to plant some winter wheat later in the season.

But Justin's words had struck a chord in him. He'd spent the summer working his butt off. Didn't he deserve a day or two to relax before his packed school schedule started up?

The screen door slammed again. Justin crossed

the porch, heading for his truck parked in the drive next to the house, Livy on his heels. She rushed out to Maddox.

"Can we go riding, pulease?"

Her puppy dog eyes and hands clasped beneath her chin made him want to laugh. He'd missed her this summer.

He shoved down the unending to-do list and chucked the front of her cowgirl hat. "You got it, princess."

"Whoohoo!"

They were crunching across the gravel toward the barn when Haley pulled in, taking the spot Justin had just vacated.

"You're not going without me, are you?" she called out as she emerged from her car.

She was usually dressed so trendy that seeing her slim jeans and T-shirt, combined with boots and a hat, struck him in the solar plexus. She looked like a real cowgirl.

"Haley's been coming out to ride with me sometimes, helping exercise the horses," Livy said as they watched her cross the yard toward them.

"Oh, don't couch it like that," Haley said with a laugh. "Livy's been giving me pointers. I think my riding is about the level of a six-year-old now."

She greeted him with an arm around his waist

and a smacking kiss on his chin that had Livy giggling.

*We need to talk.*

That boulder that had loosened as he'd considered a ride with Livy tightened up again. She probably wasn't thrilled with him after yesterday.

But her eyes were shining up at him as Livy grabbed her hand. They wheeled toward the barn, whispering and giggling together.

He followed, unable to keep from admiring how good they looked together. Livy would never know Katie, except through what he and Justin and Haley shared, but he was eternally grateful that Livy had Haley to act as a mother-figure. With only him and Justin, she'd been in dire circumstances until Haley had come around.

The ring burned in his front pocket, but he had the same concerns that had been there yesterday. Nothing had changed.

Just then, she and Livy looked over their shoulders. He should've flinched or something at the ornery look in their eyes—they were obviously planning something—but he felt only joy.

He borrowed one of Ryan's horses, so they could all ride out together, knowing his cousin wouldn't mind. Once they'd cleared the yard and moved into the field, Livy led the way in her usual exuberant fashion, galloping while her hair and a giddy laugh streamed out behind her.

Haley followed in a bouncing trot that could use a little work, and he let his mount go into a smooth lope, coming up beside her and then passing her.

For this moment in time, he felt... free.

They rode all the corners and nooks of the one hundred acre property—he saw several sections of fence that needed to be fixed—and finally led the horses down by the small pond in the back corner.

"I think I saw a quail over in this direction. I want to see if she has any chicks," Livy said, leaving her mount's reins with him.

"Don't wander too far," he said.

She rolled her eyes. "I'm not five anymore, Uncle M."

He knew. They had another two years, tops, before she figured out the whole boy-girl thing. He wasn't ready.

"Aw, I think it's cute," Haley teased. "That's what a dad is supposed to do. Worry."

Livy looked back at him, her eyes shining with moisture for the briefest moment, connecting with him in a way that hit him right in the gut. Daughter. Dad.

He winked, and she went on her curious way.

She'd been in his care since she was days old,

when his mom had been too sick with grief to care for the infant who'd lost both her parents in one fell swoop.

But he'd never openly acknowledged it—no one had—until now. Until Haley. Livy was as much his daughter as she could be.

Haley's hand slipped into his. Her opposite hand held the reins, as did his. They let the horses stand in the water, drink. It was turning out to be a scorcher again, and he was ready for cooler fall temps. He'd sweated more than he cared to admit, sitting in that combine cab for all hours of the day.

And he was sweating now for another reason.

*We need to talk.*

He swallowed hard. "I'm sorry I wasn't there for you yesterday. I should've gone with you to the closing."

She slanted a sideways look up at him. "It's okay."

He shook his head. "It's not okay. I want to be... what you need, and I wasn't that yesterday."

She let go of his hand, but instead of turning away—he had half-expected that—she wrapped her arm around his waist. He let his arm come around her shoulders, and she leaned into him as they looked out over the small pond. Her head rested in the crook of his shoulder.

"*This* is what I need. Just you."

He opened his mouth, ready to apologize again, but she went on. "I don't expect you to be Superman. I know you drove through the night yesterday and then had things waiting on you when you got to town. I'm not mad. Or hurt."

That was good. Real good. But he couldn't feel real relief, because there was still a fine tension in her, close beside him.

"I'm thinking about quitting my job."

It was the complete last thing he'd expected her to say. "What?"

"It's... hard. Being almost three hours away from you. From Livy. My heart's not in it... my heart's here. My boss has noticed that my full attention isn't on my work, and..." She sighed softly. "I think it's time to move on."

He stood dumbfounded, not sure what to say. She'd sold her late aunt's house. Now she was giving up her job. It was a lot of change, and he didn't know what to make of it.

He cleared his throat. "What will you do instead?"

She tilted her head up. From this close, looking down at her, he could count every sun-kissed freckle across the bridge of her nose.

"I've got some savings. I thought I could move into a little apartment up here. Livy's got more business than she can handle, especially once school starts. Then I'll be close enough to be here when she gets home from school. Justin's finding his feet again, it would be a shame to keep him stuck here to help with her when I can be here. A couple of folks from town have asked me about helping them market their businesses—Melody from the dress shop wants me to teach her how to build an online storefront. I figure I can do some freelancing and supplement my income."

"You want to move to Redbud Trails?" Usually people wanted to move *away* from such a small town.

"I'd be close enough to spend time with Livy. Help out. I know you'll be working long hours."

Livy. She was talking about being here for Livy. That made it a little easier to say, "I can't ask you to give up everything you'd give up to move here for Livy." Or for him. Not yet.

She turned in his embrace, now facing his chest. Her free hand played with the button at the collar of his shirt. She didn't quite meet his eyes. "I know you're not asking." She cleared her throat. "It's very obvious that you're not asking." This time, when her eyes cut up to his, he saw the vulnerability in their depths.

He raised his free hand to cup her jaw. "I want you here," he whispered fiercely, his voice choked. "I want you here so bad, but it feels like you're giving up your entire life to be with me."

Tears welled in her eyes but didn't fall. "My life, my *heart* is here. With you."

He couldn't help but kiss her, his hand sliding into her hair. She squeezed his waist and leaned into the heart-stopping kiss.

"I know it's too soon to talk about getting married," he said, breaking away, breathless. "I can't even afford a real ring. The one I have is—"

"You bought a ring?" Now her eyes were shining with joy.

"It's not much." But when it was obvious that she wasn't going to drop it, he dug into the hip pocket of his jeans and came up with the plain silver band. "It doesn't even have a rock."

She took it, sliding it on to her ring finger, bobbling the reins. "It fits."

"It fits." He couldn't believe this was happening. This was not what he'd imagined when she'd said *we need to talk*. "I guess I just need to ask, then." He took a deep breath, nerves spiraling through him even though she was giving him all green lights. "Haley, will you marry me?"

"Yes." She whispered the word, her eyes filling with tears again.

He closed her in his arms, the furthest horse

protesting with a neigh when Maddox's hold on the reins gave him a tug. Maddox dropped the reins, trusting the horses wouldn't run off and knowing they couldn't get off the property if they did.

His emotions overwhelming, too much even to kiss her, he just held her close.

"Are you guys making out *again*?" Livy's voice rang out behind them.

"No." He turned the two of them around, Haley's feet getting tangled in his boots, but he steadied her. He couldn't let her go, not yet.

"Is that a *ring*?" The exuberant joy in Livy's voice was impossible to ignore. "Yes! Yes, yes, yes!"

He couldn't help but agree with his niece's sentiments.

There were still so many obstacles to overcome. He had to get through this school year. Livy's teen years were ahead of them. Haley had to figure out her job situation.

But they would do it together. Haley wasn't leaving him. Wouldn't get tired of him.

She was his, almost for good.

*Yes, yes, yes!*

# KISSED BY A COWBOY - THE SEQUEL

# CHAPTER 1

*a* soft cry from down the hall woke Haley with a rush of her pounding heart.

She lay still in her bed, praying it'd been a dream, or a weird breath from the man sleeping soundly beside her, and not an actual cry.

Because thinking about getting out of this bed for the fourth time tonight made *her* want to cry.

A tiny wail rang out.

The man beside her slumbered on.

Haley dragged herself out of the bed, resisting the urge to punch Maddox as she padded past him. It was his fault she was in this position right now. Sleep deprived, emotional, miserable.

She pressed one hand against her lips, stifling the hysterical giggle that wanted out.

All right, it hadn't been only Maddox's fault. She'd wanted to expand their family, too.

She just hadn't known it would be like *this*.

She slipped into the upstairs bedroom and moved to the crib by memory. How many times had they done this already? Weren't they past this *getting up four times a night* stage?

It was still a few minutes before daybreak, and the room-darkening curtains would've made the room pitch-black except for a soft nightlight that created just enough illumination for her to see.

The first glimpse into the crib filled her with a burst of both joy and worry. Six-month-old Elijah was wide-awake and squirming on his back, kicking his feet.

The worry won out.

What was wrong? Was Elijah teething? She hadn't seen any signs of swollen gums, and there was only a normal amount of drool. Was it too light in here? Too dark? Was there a problem with her milk supply? The pediatrician had said not to worry about that; Elijah had measured chubby at his four-month-old checkup. But that was six weeks ago. Was he sick? He hadn't felt feverish when she'd nursed him all of two hours ago.

She'd worked herself up into a fine mettle in the few seconds it took to reach for the baby.

His pajamas were soaked through.

"Oh, monkey," she murmured. She laid her cheek briefly against the top of his head—the only dry place on him—and moved to the changing table in one corner.

His wail changed to an outraged baby-shout by the time she'd stripped the pajamas off him, wiped him down with a handful of baby wipes—she was too exhausted to put him in the tub right now—and changed his diaper.

On autopilot, she laid him carefully on the floor in the opposite corner of the room and stripped his sheets. Changing the sheets on his crib mattress was always a wrestling match, and she felt as if the crib won more than half the time. And her stress level only rose as his wails gained in volume.

*How* could Maddox sleep through this?

She was panting with exertion and had given up any hope of going back to bed by the time she'd gotten new sheets on Elijah's mattress and the mattress back inside the crib.

He was squalling when she picked him up again, red-faced with temper.

She bounced him gently in her arms, and his cries changed volume as he instinctively turned his face into her breast, nuzzling his face into the oversized T-shirt she'd worn to bed—the last clean stitch of clothes in her chest of drawers.

Exhausted tears filled her eyes as she settled into the rocking chair in the corner of the room.

They spilled over as Elijah quieted, his cries dissolving into the occasional sniffle as he nursed greedily. As if he hadn't just drunk his fill a mere two hours ago.

It wasn't the tenderness in her breasts from his over-nursing that made her cry.

How long could she keep doing this?

He wasn't a newborn any longer. He was supposed to be sleeping for longer stretches. *She* was supposed to be getting more sleep.

She hadn't slept through the night since well before the baby was born—those last few weeks of pregnancy her belly had been cumbersome and had made it impossible to get comfortable. Not to mention how many times a night she'd had to get up and pee.

She couldn't remember if she'd last showered yesterday. Or the day before.

And she couldn't keep up with the household chores. Hence, the lack of clean clothes. Today, she'd be wearing something from the dirty laundry bin, or she'd be naked.

Maybe it she walked around the house naked,

she'd be able to catch Maddox's attention. Maybe he'd finally ask her what was wrong, how he could help. Except the idea of showing him her ugly, post-baby body made her shudder.

What was wrong with her? She'd gone into motherhood believing it would be easy, she'd be a natural.

After all, she and Livy had hit it off from the beginning. As the two females in a house full of men, they'd been in each other's pockets from day one. They'd never even fought, at least not until she'd gotten pregnant with Elijah.

She'd been *so* stupid.

She was a horrible mother. She had no instincts. It had taken her well over a week to figure out this breastfeeding thing, and then only with help from a lactation consultant. They'd had multiple phone calls.

She couldn't even get Elijah to lie down for a decent nap. She'd rock him or walk him around the house for an hour before he got drowsy, and once she laid him in his crib, he'd sleep for fifteen minutes, max.

Some days, it felt impossible to love the little tyrant. She just wanted some *sleep*, darn it.

And a free hour to tackle the mountains of dishes and laundry. She didn't care about the novel she'd been in the middle of reading the day before his birth and hadn't cracked since. That was too much. She didn't even care about the dust bunnies that were crawling out from every corner. She couldn't remember the last time she'd vacuumed.

Just the dishes. Just the laundry. Just a five-hour stretch at night, and she'd feel like a new woman.

More tears spilled down her cheeks. She wiped them away with her shoulder.

She really needed to get ahold of herself.

She gazed down at the baby, who now seemed to be gnawing on her breast. *Was* he teething?

She touched one downy cheek with the pad of her finger.

She did love him. So much that it sometimes hurt her to look at him.

His eyes started to fall closed, and she couldn't help the curve of her lips that shifted into a smile. He was adorable.

She was overreacting. Par for the course since the first stirrings of pregnancy hormones.

She let her head fall back against the back of the rocker as Elijah went limp and heavy in her arms.

When she next forced her eyes open, bright June sunlight seeped in around the edges of the curtain now. Maybe if she put her pillow over her head, she could go back to sleep. It was Saturday. She thought.

She didn't have to help Livy get ready for school. Wait—it was summer. There were no family obligations today.

Thoughts of sleeping for another hour gave her just enough energy to stand up and tuck Elijah into his now-dry crib. He sucked on his lips for a brief second before his lips relaxed into a little bow.

She turned from the crib with a sense of exhausted peace.

One that promptly disappeared as she stepped into the hallway and found herself looking into Livy's bedroom—where the fourteen-year-old was climbing into the open second-story window.

MADDOX WALKED INTO A WAR ZONE.

Also known as the farmhouse kitchen.

He'd been up late last night, watching footage from the last several games his high school football team had played last fall. He coached junior high, but the high school coach was a buddy and had asked him for advice about their all-star quarterback, who would be a senior this year.

He'd also been avoiding grading the summer-school papers he'd brought home.

Why had he thought taking on a summer school class was a good idea?

155

Right. The extra money. Haley's surprise.

All he wanted was a cup of coffee to jolt him awake, but he walked into the kitchen in his sock feet to find his niece-turned-daughter facing off with his wife.

They were whisper-shouting at each other.

"Where is this even coming from?" Haley demanded, her voice low. She was adorably tousled, her hair mussed and a giant T-shirt—his T-shirt?—rumpled to mid-thigh. She glanced at him briefly and then back at Livy.

He sent one longing look at the coffeepot. It was empty, not even percolating.

"What do you care?" Livy returned in a whisper. She was already dressed in a tank top and jeans, her hair French-braided. She threw her hands up, and he caught sight of the black-painted nails he hated.

They needed one of those single-cup coffee makers. His brother had one. Justin could make himself the perfect cup in under a minute.

Haley finally noticed his presence in the kitchen. Her eyes lit, and it wasn't a welcoming kind of light.

More like, she was getting ready to throw him into the middle of whatever this fight was.

"Maddox, why don't you ask Livy where she was all night? Because she sure wasn't in her bed."

He'd been heading to the coffeepot, his need for

caffeine trumping whatever little thing had them riled up at each other, but Haley's words froze him to the spot.

He spun on his heel to level a look at his daughter.

There might've been a speck of guilt, but it was quickly hidden behind Livy's stubborn chin-raise. "So what?"

His job as a teacher and coach meant he was around junior high school kids all day long. On game days, even longer.

He was used to emotional outbursts, crude jokes, even occasionally being cursed out.

But he was never going to get used to Livy's attitude.

He worked to keep his voice down, knowing the baby was sleeping upstairs. "You know the rules. You have a curfew."

She shrugged. "I was in my room at curfew. You saw me."

He had. He'd said goodnight and blown her a kiss from the hallway as he'd snuck to his own bedroom, knowing Haley needed her sleep.

"No sneaking out after curfew is implied."

A ten-year-old Livy would've dissolved into tears, upset that she'd disappointed him. She would've burrowed into his arms for a hug amidst sobbing and apologies.

This teenaged Livy didn't do any of that. She stared him down, temper sparking in her eyes. "I can take care of myself. It's not like I was out at Croeger's Point."

The thought of her visiting the make-out spot sparked a pulse of pain behind his right eye.

"How do we know that?" Haley interrupted, even though she'd pushed him into the middle of this argument.

The pain behind his eye pulsed hotter.

"If you're not where you're supposed to be, you could be anywhere. Even laying in a ditch, dead."

The pain behind his eye burst into a full-fledged headache.

"Enough." He sliced one hand through the air, silencing both of them.

Livy crossed her arms over her chest, her entire posture speaking defiance.

He pointed one finger at her. "Go to your room. We're tabling this discussion for now."

She whirled on her heel.

"And stay in there," he called after her.

She didn't respond.

When he turned to Haley—who stood just in

front of the coffeepot—her eyes were sparking with temper too.

What?

"You can't let her off easy," his wife said. "Not for something like this."

He reached for her, but she pushed his arm away before he could pull her into a hug. Even though she looked like she needed a hug.

Apparently, she didn't want one.

He reached for the coffeepot instead, removing the carafe to fill it with water.

"I'm not going to," he said.

She stomped to the fridge. "You always let her off easy."

Always. That was a bit of an exaggeration.

Before he could say anything else, a door overhead slammed. Livy's door.

Haley's wide-eyed glance went to the ceiling.

And as if that were his cue, Elijah wailed.

Haley buried her head in her hands. He thought she might be laughing, but a soft sob escaped.

"Hey—"

Her shoulders rose as she inhaled a deep, shaky breath. Obviously trying to contain whatever emotion was overwhelming her.

"I'll get Elijah," he said. "He's probably hungry, right?"

Whatever splinter of calm Haley had grabbed onto, his words obliterated it. She broke down into sobs, her shoulders shaking.

"Hey," he said again. He pulled her into his arms. What was this? His wife was usually unflappable. There'd been some crying jags in the first weeks after the baby was born, but this...

Was kinda scary.

"It'll be okay." He rubbed a circle on her back.

She shook her head in response. Tried to edge away. "I h—have to go get him."

"I'll get him. Take a few minutes."

She leaned on him for the barest of moments before she let go, turning to reach for a paper towel from the roll on the counter.

He felt helpless in the face of her noisy tears.

*a*fter Haley had calmed slightly, Maddox went upstairs and picked up Elijah, who stopped crying and shoved his little fist in his mouth. Maddox patted the baby's diaper and found it dry.

Elijah seemed content nestled against his shoulder, so Maddox chose to brave the lion's den. Aka Livy's room. He knocked on the door she'd slammed earlier.

She didn't answer.

She'd had a thing about privacy lately, which meant he couldn't just barge in her room.

But didn't breaking the rules mean her privileges should be revoked?

He rapped once more. "Livy, I'm coming in." He opened the door.

"Geez, Uncle Maddox!" She was lying on top of her quilt, fully dressed, one arm thrown over her face. "I'm trying to sleep."

"Too bad." It wasn't even seven yet, but Livy had always loved early mornings on the farm. The old Livy had, anyway. Lately, he'd had to drag her out there to do chores. "Where were you this morning?"

"Nowhere."

Okay, so they were doing this the hard way.

"You're already grounded for a week."

She groaned.

On his shoulder, Elijah snuffled. Maddox rubbed a circle on his little back. "If you don't want to make it two, tell me where you were."

His threat passed right over her. She rolled over, pulling her pillow over her head.

Okay, then.

He moved to the edge of her bed and nudged her thigh with his knee. "Get up."

"Go away."

She still hadn't looked him in the face, not since the stare-down in the kitchen. He'd known her since she was born, had custody of her—had been her dad —since she was a few weeks old. He figured if he could see her face, he'd know what kind of trouble she'd gotten into last night.

"Livy."

Still no response.

This time he tugged the pillow away.

For a brief second, he caught sight of the little girl who'd played this game and then dissolved into a tickle-war. But her eyes met his, and for a split second, her face crumpled as if she was going to cry, too.

The expression was gone so quickly he might've imagined it. She donned a mulish expression, haughty with defiance, and he was done.

"Get up. Put your shoes on."

She grumbled under her breath but finally got up off the bed. He didn't know how she found them amongst the crap spread across her floor, but she snatched her worn pair of Justin boots and shoved her feet into them.

"Mucking stalls isn't real punishment, you know." She mumbled the words beneath her breath.

And he was reminded of a time when he'd been nine or ten. Old enough he should've known better. He'd gotten a spanking from his dad for some unremembered act of disobedience. And fired off *"that didn't even hurt."*

Right about now he understood the flash of temper he'd seen in his dad's eyes and why he hadn't been able to sit down right for the better part of a week.

Of course, he'd never had any desire to parent the way his drunk of a father had. Which meant he stuffed his first reaction, gritting his teeth to get the words out.

"You're right. After chores, we'll get to the real deal."

She flicked one glance at him, then crossed her arms and preceded him out of the room and down the hall.

Seriously.

Did she think he was joking?

Haley had already told him not to go easy on her.

"Do they both think I'm a pushover?" he asked the sleeping baby drooling through his T-shirt.

Downstairs, Livy was already heading out the back door, not looking back. She let the screen door slam behind her, and Elijah jumped at the noise, but Maddox quickly rubbed his back, and Elijah settled back down into sleep.

Haley stood at the now-spotless counter, sponge in hand. The dishes that had been overflowing the sink, the ones he'd planned to do himself this morning, had disappeared, and the dishwasher was humming along.

Her eyes were red-rimmed, but she looked at him expectantly.

He eyed the coffeepot and its fragrant brew,

wondering whether he dared ask her to pour him a mug. Better do it himself.

"Well?" she asked.

"Grounded for two weeks," he said. How's that for *too easy*? "Plus, after chores, I'm going to take her up to the school and have her clean out the locker rooms."

Haley's nose wrinkled at that, but she didn't disagree.

He took that as a good sign and edged toward the coffeepot. He took down an extra-large travel mug and set it on the counter. He wasn't as good as Haley had gotten at this one-handed stuff, but he managed to fill the mug without bobbling the baby or spilling any of the steaming liquid. He didn't doctor it. Today was a black coffee kind of day.

"Did she say where she'd been?" Haley asked, her gaze going out the window toward the barn. She shook her head. "Sneaking out is just not like her."

"No, but it's like Katie." His sister had been the wild child. Come to think of it, his brother Justin had been wild too. Somehow Maddox had ended up the stick in the mud of the three.

A sad smile quickly passed over Haley's face.

He wanted to see more of her smile.

"I thought I could take the little guy with me," he

said. "I figure if I time it right, he'll nap most of the time."

Haley wasn't smiling. Her brows were crunched over her eyes. "You don't need to do that. I'm fine." But the flatness of her statement told him very clearly that she wasn't.

He racked his brain. She'd only let loose of the baby enough for Maddox to keep him by himself once. Maybe twice, when she'd run to the grocery store. No wonder she needed a break.

"I want to. That way you can relax—maybe take a nap—before your book club friends come over this afternoon."

She froze, and some internal alarm went off inside him as she turned panicked eyes on him.

"What?"

He almost took a step back at the fire in her eyes.

"Your book club," he said, not having to act dumb. Had she forgotten? "Coupla weeks ago, you said you really missed going to the book club meetings. And I said you should have the next one here." She'd agreed with him.

But now her eyes had gone a little wild. "I only said 'sure' hypothetically. As in, 'sure, that'd be fun in about three years.'"

He didn't get what the big deal was.

She ran both hands down her face. "Okay. Okay.

But I never mentioned it to Karlie. And you never mentioned it to her, either..."

Her voice trailed off as she looked up at him and, no doubt, caught the guilty look he was sporting.

"I called her," he said. "Because you said you wanted to have book club here."

Her hands flew above her head. "I don't want to have book club here! Have you seen the house?"

She pointed to the living room, and his gaze followed her gesture. He could see one of the throw pillows on the floor and several baby toys that had escaped the toy basket in the corner of the room.

He shrugged. "It won't take long to tidy up. I'll help, if you want."

Her eyes drifted skyward. Like maybe she was asking for help from above.

"I haven't dusted in months. Haven't vacuumed in two weeks. Our house is a disaster."

He shrugged. "Nobody cares about that stuff."

Maybe that wasn't the right thing to say, because her eyes went a little wider, a little wilder. She plucked the material of the shirt she wore and pulled it away from her body. "Do you see this shirt? This was the last clean piece of clothing in the entire house."

Now, he knew that was an exaggeration. Elijah

had a closet full of clean baby clothes. And probably under all her junk, Livy had some clean clothes too.

"You haven't gone shopping in months," he said. "Why not visit the dress shop in town and get yourself something new?"

She laughed, the sound slightly hysterical. He thought he saw a sheen of tears in her eyes before she blinked. She waved off that suggestion without even considering it. "I can't even keep up with the dishes and laundry, and you want me to host book club?"

"I don't want you to do anything," he tried. "You said—"

"I know!" Her volume had gone to a decibel that exacerbated his headache.

Elijah stirred in his arms. He jiggled the baby. "Do you want me to call Karlie and cancel? Or, you know what, if you called Ashley, I bet she and her mom would bring some snacks."

Haley had gone from looking wild to looking defeated. "You go do your thing. I'll figure something out."


"WHAT DID you think about the hero's motivation, Haley?"

Haley startled from where she was nodding off,

tucked in the corner of the couch. Next to her, Ashley—Maddox's cousin Ryan's wife—was fingering the pages of the open novel. Ten women were scattered around her living room, and as all their gazes rested on her, Haley felt a bubble of anxiety burst in her chest.

"I think... I need something to drink. Will you skip my turn?"

She excused herself, knowing she'd been rude. She rushed into the kitchen anyway.

This book club meeting was a disaster. No, *she* was the disaster.

She padded across to the fridge, bypassing the cute little mini-cheesecakes and cut up fruit that Ashley's mom had made. Haley'd taken Maddox's advice and made the phone call, even though it made her feel like even more of a failure.

She took a can of soda out of the fridge and stood by the counter, pressing the cold aluminum to her temple. She didn't need the calories, that was for sure, but right now she craved the taste.

"Hey. Everything okay?"

She startled at the quiet question from behind her.

Ash.

Her cousin-in-law stood on the opposite side of the island, snagging a strawberry. She and Haley had been close for so long that Haley didn't really see her disability anymore—she'd lost most of her right arm on her last tour of duty. Haley only saw the woman.

Ash popped the bit of fruit into her mouth, waiting for Haley's answer.

She pasted on a smile. "I'm fine."

Ash's gaze narrowed. "Liar."

Haley sighed. The other woman had been all prickles and independence when she'd fallen for Ryan, Maddox's cousin. When they'd gotten engaged and Ash had admitted she didn't have any close girl-friends, no one to be her maid of honor, Haley had pushed her way into the other woman's life. They'd become best friends.

And of course, Ash wasn't going to let her *I'm fine* stand.

She tried another one. "I'm just tired."

It was true, but it wasn't all of it. She'd been tired from the moment she woke up. She'd spent the morning deep-cleaning the living room, kitchen, and downstairs bathroom and praying that no one went into other parts of the house.

By the time Maddox had returned with Livy and the baby, Haley had been painfully engorged, and Elijah had been red-faced and squalling. He'd clung to her while she'd stuffed herself with leftovers from last night's roast, standing up at the counter.

Maddox and Livy had made themselves scarce as the first of the ladies had arrived.

Haley'd been running on fumes by that time. And now even her fumes were running dry.

"I'm just glad you made it to the meeting." Ash played with a stack of napkins on the counter, fanning them out. "I hate being the only one in there under forty."

Haley snorted. It was true, the group ran more to women who were friends with Ash's mom.

"I didn't read this month's book," she confessed. She remembered the fateful conversation with Maddox a couple of days after missing last month's meeting, but she hadn't given the club another thought since that day.

Ashley looked up, her eyes sparkling. "Me neither."

They shared a smile that turned into a giggle that quickly turned into tears on Haley's side.

Embarrassed, she turned away, blindly reaching for the roll of paper towels next to the fridge.

"Hey, what's wrong?" She heard Ash's footsteps as the other woman rounded the island.

She quickly dabbed at the tears on her face. Tried for an upbeat tone. "I'm just tired," she repeated.

Tired. Overwhelmed. Failing at being a mom.

Her tears came faster. She was becoming a regular watering pot.

Ash wrapped her arm around Haley's shoulders as she cried into her paper towel.

"Elijah h-hasn't been s-sleeping," she said, voice wobbling.

Ash gave her a squeeze. "Is he teething?"

"I don't know!"

"Haley, Annabel wants to know—oh my." Ash's mom Mary trailed off, and Haley put more effort into getting herself under control.

She heard Mary murmur something to the ladies in the living room, but her voice was pitched too low to make out the words. And then moments later, another pair of arms came around her.

"It's okay, honey. Whatever it is, we're here for you," said Mary.

That threatened to set her off again.

"Elijah might be teething," Ashley said, her words reverberating above Haley's head.

Mary patted her shoulder, and the two women eased back as Haley's cries settled into sniffles.

"I can't actually tell," Haley said, voice still wobbling. She dabbed at her eyes with the same paper towel, now nearly shredded.

Ash tore a new one off the roll and handed it to her.

"Thanks. He h-hasn't had a fever and he's only chewing on stuff—his hand, his toys—a little bit. But he's not sleeping at night. What if something else is wrong?"

Mary didn't make fun of her for speaking the fear aloud. "You know, I remember when Ashley came to us."

Right. Ashley had been adopted.

"She was a little younger than your Elijah," Mary went on. "And the social worker brought her to us and then—" She clapped her hands, making Haley jump. —"she just left. She just walked out and left me and Joe with this tiny infant."

Ashley smiled a bittersweet smile at the mention of her father, who'd passed away last year.

"That first year, I was scared of everything. Every little fever. Every time she cried, I asked myself, 'Was that a different cry? Is she in pain? What's wrong?'"

She reached out and patted Haley's shoulder. "That anxiety you're feeling is normal."

It was?

"I think every new parent is scared they're going to do the wrong thing. Feed the baby something they're allergic to. Ruin their sleeping habits. Drop them. There's a lot you've got to get right."

Beside her, Ash had gone pale. Her hand was pressed against her collarbone.

"But most parents have good instincts. Trust yourself." Mary glanced at Ashley, then looked longer. "Honey, what's wrong?"

Ash had gone from pale to green.

"Are you okay?" Haley asked her friend.

Ash nodded slowly. Shook her head. "I'm terrified right now."

Haley laughed softly. "Why?"

"Because I'm pregnant."

Mary's eyes went wide, and then she started to smile. "Oh, honey."

Haley had regained enough equilibrium to feel joy for her best friend. "Ash!"

She moved out of the way as Mary hugged her daughter. When she moved back, she wiped a tear from her eye.

Haley took her turn giving Ash a hug.

"Don't... I haven't told Ryan yet. I'm just barely past my missed period, but I'd been feeling really nauseous in the mornings so I took a test..."

Ash did look freaked out, her eyes haunted.

It was Haley's turn to reassure her friend. "You'll be a great mom. Don't look at me as an example."

Mary had her hands clasped beneath her chin. "Ryan is going to be thrilled. That boy..."

Haley couldn't help but grin. Ryan could be a

jokester sometimes, though he worked harder than anyone else she knew, except maybe Maddox.

But Ash wasn't smiling. "Keep it a secret for now, okay? I've got to find the right way to tell him."

The other book club ladies chose that moment to converge on them, and they lost the chance for further discussion.

But as Haley saw the women off and Elijah started kicking up a fuss upstairs, she slumped against the front door.

Was this emotional exhaustion normal? Was she really normal?

Because she still felt like a failure.

CHAPTER 3

*J*t was a few minutes before dawn the next morning, and Maddox was folding laundry in the living room when Haley peered through the kitchen doorway.

"Hey," he greeted her softly. He flipped up the kitchen towel with a quick snap of his wrist and folded it into fourths, then added it to a growing pile on the end table next to the couch.

She padded into the room, hair adorably tousled and wearing one of his old T-shirts over a pair of sweatpants.

He folded her into his arms, burying his nose in her hair, breathing her in. She smelled like her honey-flavored shampoo and woman, with a hint of baby wipes.

"I heard noise down here. Thought it might be

Livy again. What're you doing?" she asked into his shoulder, her words hot against his skin.

"Helping."

Until yesterday, he hadn't realized how selfish he'd been with his time. How hard was it to throw in an extra load of laundry while he watched TV before bed? Easy. Get up fifteen minutes early and fold it? He was used to early mornings.

He hated himself a little for not noticing how completely overwhelmed his wife had been.

He could care less if he had to scrub his cereal bowl by hand before he used it, or if he had to pull a clean T-shirt out of the dryer to wear for the day.

But if those things bothered Haley, he was going to see to it that they were fixed. Even if that meant forgoing an hour of sleep every day.

He wanted her to be happy. For a while, before Elijah, he'd thought they'd had it made.

He'd gotten complacent.

Stupid.

But with Haley nestled in his arms, where she belonged, maybe he could fix it.

"I don't want you to have to do my chores," she mumbled.

He ducked his head to kiss her temple, her cheek, the corner of her mouth. He let his nose run along the line of her jaw. "I don't mind," his whispered against her skin.

Her hands rested at his waist. Squeezed when he bent his head to kiss the place where his T-shirt met her neck. "Well, I do." Her voice emerged breathless, and he felt a surge of manly pride that he'd made her react.

He'd missed this closeness with her since the baby's arrival.

He lifted his head to kiss her mouth, but she blocked him by turning her head to the side. "I'm serious. I don't want you to take on more work around here. It's not fair to you."

He used one finger at her chin to turn her head to him. He slanted his lips across hers, the heat of her mouth like coming home. Still. Even after three years. He let his tongue stroke the bow of her upper lip, but she broke away with a gasp just when things were getting good.

Her hands had come up to clutch his shoulders, and she gave a little push and pulled completely away from him. "Quit trying to distract me."

He hadn't been, not really. But got another surge of pride that he was able to do so.

"You work hard enough." He could tell by the stubborn set of her lips that they were going to talk about this, whether he wanted to or not.

She turned away to pick up something out of the shrinking pile of clean laundry on the couch.

He came up behind her, set one hand on her hip. Brushed a couple wayward strands of hair behind her ear. "Honey, there's no reason for you to keep struggling when I can help."

From the side, he saw the flare of her nostrils, knew she had some ready comeback for that. He rushed on.

"There are no *your chores* or *my chores* around here. Who do you think did the dishes before we got married?"

"Justin." Her sassy mention of his brother made him smile. She snapped a tiny shirt—Elijah's—in the air before folding it neatly.

"I'm gonna be helping more around here. And Livy should be helping more, too."

She pulled a face.

He chuckled. "She might disagree at first. But you need to rest more, so between the two of us, we'll pick up some of the slack."

"I'm fine."

After the breakdown she'd had yesterday, he wanted to disagree. She wasn't fine. Things around here needed to change.

But she had stopped arguing about the chores,

and maybe that was enough for now. He still had Cancun up his sleeve.

He wanted to go back to the hot kiss they'd just shared.

She matched and folded a tiny pair of socks, then tossed them into a pile in the corner of the couch. When she straightened, he let both hands rest on her shoulders. His thumbs swept a line up her neck, and she leaned back against him.

He brushed a kiss against her jaw, pressed his cheek to hers as his arms came around her more fully.

She was turning her head to meet his kiss as his hands moved from her hips to rest on her belly.

Before he could say *let's go upstairs*, she jumped away, breaking his hold on her.

"Haley—"

She was heading toward the kitchen, but judging by her rapid stride, he didn't think she was inviting him to follow.

"I thought I heard the baby." She threw the words over her shoulder, but she didn't meet his gaze.

And she left him standing there, befuddled and hot under the collar. He would have sworn she'd been responding to his caresses. That she'd wanted the closeness, the intimacy, they hadn't shared in way too long.

Even if Elijah had woken up crying, so what? The baby could wait, couldn't he?

Maybe a mom didn't think so.

But there was a part of him that recognized that her words as she'd run away were an excuse.

They really needed Cancun.

# CHAPTER 4

*H*aley was watching the clock late Monday afternoon.

Maddox should've been home by now. The summer school dismissal bell would've rung at three-thirty. She knew he liked to clean up and get his next day's lesson plan in order. Today he'd taken Livy with him to give Haley a break from the teen's snark. No doubt she'd whined the entire afternoon, stuck in her dad's classroom with a book.

Haley'd been surprised and disappointed when Maddox had taken on the summer class without telling her. She'd wanted the long summer days to spend together as a family. They'd still have some. There was a month's break between the summer class and fall semester. Some, but not enough.

Where were they? It was almost six-thirty now,

and the dinner she'd actually cared about cooking was getting cold.

It was meant to be an apology.

She'd known exactly where things were heading Saturday morning. She'd been doing her best to ignore the fact that she had bedhead and morning breath and hadn't shaved her legs in over a week. And then he'd put his hands on her stomach.

Her flabby, post-childbirth, still-hanging-onto-twenty-pounds stomach.

And whatever sparks she'd been feeling had been doused with ice-cold water.

She felt bad about running away, but everything combined had killed the mood. Especially her body.

She knew she needed to hit the gym. Or go jogging. Or something.

But she was just so tired. All the time. And the minutes she had to herself in between feeding, diapering, and caring for the baby were few and far between.

But she also hated that she'd disappointed her husband.

On Saturday, she'd spent a few hours rushing through a deep clean of the house.

Today, it was a deep clean of herself.

Instead of using the dry shampoo she used more often than not, she'd taken a real shower. Shaved her legs. Put on perfume and makeup. Curled her hair.

And beneath the floor-length maxi-dress, she'd squeezed into the cutest panties and bra she could fit into.

She was trying to ignore the fact that squeezing into them had created bulges that hadn't been there pre-pregnancy.

It was too late to do anything about her body, at least for today. Once Livy and the baby had gone to bed, she and Maddox could too. And as long as the light was out, she'd try to overcome the horrible self-consciousness she felt.

Just one problem.

Her husband hadn't shown up to eat the steak dinner that was now going cold.

And then, finally, she caught sight of a plume of dust that heralded a vehicle coming up the driveway.

She glanced at Elijah, dozing off in his swing tucked in beside the table in the breakfast nook.

"Here we go," she breathed.

She put on the most welcoming smile she could and leaned one shoulder against the backdoor jamb, striking what she hoped was a casual pose.

Livy was coming up fast, but Haley looked past her to Maddox. He hadn't looked her way yet, had rounded the back of the truck to pull something out of the truck bed.

"Guess what?" Livy called out before her boots hit the porch steps. "Dad got me a puppy!"

The words didn't register at first.

And when they did, when Haley glanced up and saw the furry bundle clutched against Livy's chest, the bottom dropped out of her stomach.

Maddox did *what*?

Livy bounded up the steps and turned so that Haley got face-to-furry nose with the black and white furball in her arms.

"Isn't she so cute?"

Haley didn't know whether she murmured assent or just grunted. Livy didn't seem to need her acknowledgement, because she breezed right into the house.

Maddox was coming up the porch steps now. And if his smile was a little tired, he deserved it, didn't he? He was the one who'd gotten up early for the laundry's sake.

"You look nice," he said.

His arms were full of a dog bed and other puppy detritus. Squeaky toys.

Just perfect for waking up a sleeping baby.

What was she supposed to do with a puppy?

Every nice thought she'd had about Maddox today was erased in a rush of anger.

She turned on her heel and let the screen door slam in his face.

A puppy? What was he thinking? Like she needed any more work to do around here.

It was as if he'd already forgotten his promises from the other morning.

She was trembling with anger as she stalked back to the table, where the cooling food was looking more and more like canned dog food.

But she took a breath. Maybe this was fixable. He could just take it back. If she went all banshee on him, he might have a knee jerk reaction, and she'd end up with the dog anyway.

"Food's getting cold," she called out, keeping her voice as even as she could manage.

"Just a minute." Maddox was rustling around in the laundry room. Livy was holding the puppy up for Elijah to see—even though the baby was sleeping —when he emerged with an empty laundry tub and a worn towel.

"We can trap her in here while we eat, then we'll get everything settled after dinner."

"Wash your hands, please," Haley tacked on.

Livy gave only a minor eye roll before she complied. She was bubbly and chatty—mostly with the puppy—as she got her settled in his basket and took her seat at the table.

"This looks great," Maddox said as he sat in the chair across the table.

She hummed noncommittally. The steaks and potatoes had tasted great an hour ago, when she'd expected him. Her smile felt brittle enough to fall off her face.

"How was your afternoon at the school?" she asked Livy.

She expected to hear how boring it had been, that Maddox had made her sit and read or doodle or whatever, but instead Livy practically bounced in her chair.

"I met the new Vice Principal."

"Oh, yeah?"

"Yeah. This is her first VP job, and when Mrs. Heller"—the junior high principal—"asked Dad to show her around, I got to be in charge of his whole class!"

Leaving a future ninth grader to supervise a bunch of her peers sounded like a recipe for trouble, but Maddox seemed unconcerned as he cut into his steak.

Livy had called him Dad. It went to show just how much her attitude had changed—at least toward him. Two days ago, it had been *Uncle Maddox*.

"And she's really pretty and I got to help her unpack some of her boxes in her new office and she's traveled all over the world, even Paris!"

Livy's chatter had gone over Haley's head. Except for the *really pretty* part. She looked up from her food.

"She's not Mrs. Heller's age?"

Mrs. Heller was in her mid-fifties with gray hair sprayed and styled into a helmet around her head. She was tall and statuesque and strict and had grandkids in elementary school.

Maddox was studiously slathering butter on his potato. It was Livy who answered.

"No, she's cool. She's like your age, except she's not married."

So the new vice principal was young, single, and *really pretty?*

And Haley's husband was one of two men who worked at the junior high—the other one was a janitor her dad's age.

"And after class was dismissed me and Dad helped her lug this really heavy shelf from her car into her office."

Maddox pointed his roll at Livy. "It wasn't that heavy."

She giggled.

Showing someone around was one thing. But

moving furniture went a little above the call of duty, didn't it?

Haley knew the jealousy spreading through her with its insidious tentacles probably wasn't entirely rational, but... Maddox was a man. A handsome man with a soft heart and that devastating smile.

And all she could think about was how she'd blown him off.

MADDOX HAD THOUGHT Haley might have to warm up to the idea of a new dog in the house, but he hadn't expected the level of fury she was unleashing on the innocent frying pan she was scrubbing in the sink.

"Why don't you let me clean up?" he asked.

He edged in close behind her and cupped her shoulders in his hands.

She shrugged him off. "Oh, I think you've done enough today."

Ouch. Yeah, she was steamed.

Good thing he'd sent Livy and the puppy outside for a walk before bed. He figured Livy would detour to the barn, which gave him at least a half hour to grovel his way back into Haley's good graces.

He leaned against the counter at her side, facing her.

She stared at the sudsy pan, still scrubbing it angrily with her sponge.

"I'm sorry I didn't call and ask what you thought about the puppy," he said.

He could only hope his end-of-summer surprise would receive a better reception.

"I thought we agreed Livy needed to be punished," she said through gritted teeth. "You *rewarded* her." She shook her head, blowing a gust of air. Either she was trying to get some wayward strands of hair out of her eyes, or she was so fired up she couldn't even find words to blast him with.

Or both.

"It's not a reward."

She sent him an *oh, yeah?* glare at that.

"A kid needs a dog around. It makes for a happy childhood."

Emmie, their huge black farm dog, had died almost a year ago, and he'd been feeling the absence for a while. Livy had brought up getting a puppy several times over the last couple of months. And when Ryan had heard about this new litter of Border Collies and called Maddox, it had seemed like the perfect time.

"And who do you think is going to take care of this puppy? What about training? What if he bites Elijah?"

He wasn't that worried about it. In his experience, dogs—even puppies—had a sixth sense when it came to babies. Didn't mean he wasn't going to watch the puppy like a hawk when Elijah was on the floor, but he wasn't worried about it.

"Livy will take care of the puppy. She's old enough."

Haley parked her sudsy hands on her hips. The skeptical attitude shouldn't have been sexy, but it was. Or maybe he'd just been without her for too long.

"I promise, everything will work out." He set his hands over hers and nudged her close enough that their knees bumped.

She didn't lose the attitude.

He laced their fingers together. "If Livy needs help, I'll take care of it. And as to training, we'll get in one of Ash's obedience classes."

Ryan's wife was a local dog training guru. She held classes at the feed store a couple of times a week. They were always packed with locals and dog owners from the nearest counties.

"If it barks and whines in the night, it's gone," she mumbled, staring at his chest.

She was softening.

He untangled their fingers and skimmed his

hands up her sides. Back down. He pulled her closer and slid his arms around her lower back.

"You're still a pushover," she said.

But she didn't seem to mind too much as she nestled into his embrace.

"Am not." He rubbed his chin against her jaw. "Is this makeup you're wearing for me?"

He'd noticed the floor-length dress, too. Couldn't remember seeing it before. Maybe it was new.

He watched in fascination as a blotch of pink appeared where her neck met her shoulder. Then another just below her ear. The blush climbed all the way into her face. He leaned back to watch.

She wouldn't meet his eyes.

"I know I've let myself go since the baby was born—"

He shushed her with a gentle finger against her lips. He removed it and let his hand slide behind her head, into her hair. "You're beautiful. With makeup on or without it."

Her eyes cut to the side, as if she didn't believe what he was saying but she didn't want to disagree. She bit her lip.

"Beautiful," he repeated.

And then he kissed her.

She didn't hesitate. She deepened the kiss, opening to him like a flower to the sun.

And the back door banged open.

He stopped kissing her but didn't let go at the sound of nails scrabbling on the kitchen tiles. As far as he was concerned, Livy could take the puppy upstairs to her bedroom.

But when the screen door slammed behind her, Elijah startled and woke with a wail.

Haley went on red-alert, her entire body tensing. And not in a good way.

He sighed and let her go.

Not tonight, buddy.

# CHAPTER 5

"*A*nd how are we doing today? Six months already. Hard to believe."

Haley looked down at Elijah, nestled in her lap wearing only his diaper. The nurse had already been in the brightly-colored exam room and taken his measurements and temperature. It'd only been a week since Maddox and Livy had brought the puppy home.

"We're all right," she told the doctor.

"Hmm. You don't sound sure." He sat on a rolling stool, his white coat falling open to reveal slacks and a dress shirt beneath. He was relaxed and smiling, a man around her dad's age. She'd initially liked him because of his experience.

"I thought he'd be sleeping through the night by now," she admitted.

Elijah gurgled, chewing on his fist.

"Well, he's plenty old enough. How many times is he up during the night? Is he nursing?"

"Yes. Sometimes twice, sometimes three times." *I feel like a zombie.*

The doctor wheeled to the computer on a desk in the corner. "Let's look and see..." He tapped away at the keys and the monitor flicked to life. Another few keystrokes. "He's in the fifty-third percentile for his weight and height. He certainly doesn't look like he's missing any meals."

Haley looked down at the chub that rolled the edge of the baby's diaper.

"Does he have any teeth coming in?"

She shrugged miserably. "I can't tell. He chews on everything, but I haven't been able to see or feel a tooth coming through the gums."

He smiled at her. A patient smile. Maybe one that carried a little bit of humoring her. "Babies cry, Mrs. Michaels. At night. During the day. All the time. It's okay to let him cry himself to sleep."

She inhaled quickly, a gut reaction. Let Elijah cry? On purpose?

"Isn't that cruel?" she asked.

Now she felt sure the doctor's smile was descending into condescension. "Not at all. Babies need to learn to self-soothe."

195

That sounded reasonable. Except..." I want him to know I'm nearby. That I love him." Was that so wrong? "I don't want him to be afraid."

"You're his mother. It's your choice, of course. I'm just telling you that you can choose to let him self-soothe. It might be healthy for you both."

She tried to return his smile, but her expression felt fragile, false.

"Let's check Elijah out, if you don't mind." He now scooted his chair across the floor until his knees almost touched hers. He pulled his stethoscope from around his neck and plugged the ends into his ears. He buffed the diaphragm on his shirt before he placed it on Elijah's chest to listen.

She sat motionless as he went through the exam. Listened to Elijah's heart and lungs, looked in his eyes, ears, and mouth, tested his hip joints.

All the while, his words ran circles through Haley's brain. *Let him self-soothe. Healthy for the both of you.*

It couldn't be that easy, could it?

Like there was anything easy about letting her sweet child cry in his bed while she listened.

The doctor finally sat back. "He looks great. Any other questions?"

She shook her head dumbly. Was she harming her son? Or would it damage him if she let him cry?

But the doctor didn't get up off his stool. "How are you doing, Mom?"

Her gaze snapped up to him. "I'm fine." She gave the rote answer she gave to everyone.

He held her gaze.

And her face began to grow hot.

"I'm fine—mostly," she admitted. She hadn't come in here intending to admit any such thing. "My... my emotions are all over the place. I think it's from lack of sleep, but..." To her consternation, tears welled in her eyes.

"You're breastfeeding, right?"

She nodded.

"It's common for breastfeeding mothers to notice their hormones aren't completely back to normal until the baby weans."

Seriously?

"I thought—I mean, I read six to eight weeks."

He shrugged. "For some women. No two moms are the same." He crossed his arms. "Are you experiencing any thoughts of harming yourself or the baby? Detachment issues?"

She shook her head. "No."

"I don't think it's postpartum depression. Do you have any reason to think that's what you're experiencing?"

"It hadn't even occurred to me."

Her tears began to dissipate at his calm manner.

He looked at her awhile longer. Then stood up. "I'm going to have the nurse print some information for you while she's preparing the vaccinations for Elijah here. One of the things is the information for a support group for new moms. It meets at the local library every other Tuesday. I think you'd benefit from attending."

She didn't know if she could face other women. Not when she was certain they must have known what they were doing—at least much more than she did.

But she smiled and shook the doctor's hand anyway.

TEN MINUTES after they'd left the doctor's office, Haley found herself pushing a happy Elijah in his stroller down the empty halls of Redbud Trails Junior High.

She'd descended so low... but she couldn't forget Livy's remarks about the new vice principal... *really pretty.*

Or ignore the fact that Maddox had been arriving home later than usual every day.

Plus, there was her failed seduction. After the disastrous dinner, she'd fully intended to be awake when Maddox had come to bed, but she'd fallen asleep with the lights on.

He hadn't mentioned it the next morning.

She'd tried to tell herself she was being a jealous idiot, yet here she was, stalking the halls of a nearly deserted junior high on the search for a gorgeous wife-stealing school administrator and questioning her own sanity.

The dismissal bell had rung at least fifteen minutes ago, and there was no sign of any kids. They'd already vacated the building. Livy had begged to stay home with her puppy, bored at the mere idea of sitting through Elijah's pediatrician appointment with Haley. So Haley was alone on this adventure.

She turned the corner to the hallway where Maddox's classroom was located. As it was on the interior of the building, the entire hallway was dim. Lights off. From here, she could see that his door was closed and no light shone around the edges.

Maybe he was in the tiny coach's office next to the locker rooms.

But after trekking down another two hallways, pushing the stroller, she found that empty too.

Where was he?

She'd parked next to his truck outside in the teacher lot. He would've recognized her car and waited for her, if he'd gone out that way. And she hadn't seen anyone since she'd entered the building.

This had been such a dumb idea.

She retraced her steps to leave. No one had to know she'd been here at all.

But as she passed dark, silent classrooms, voices sounded. A laugh.

In the middle of the building, two major hallways crossed. She took a look to her left. There was a light on.

The teacher's lounge.

Maybe it wasn't him. Maddox had always professed that when his students left for the day, he was ready to come home to her, to his family. If he wasn't in his classroom finishing up from the day or preparing for tomorrow's work, could he really be in there... *visiting?*

*Go home.* There was a part of her that wanted to bury her head in the sand and pretend. Maddox loved her. He wouldn't have an affair.

Would he?

In the three years they'd been married, he'd never taken on a summer school class. Not until this year.

She had to know.

She pushed the stroller toward the one lighted doorway, wincing at each squeak of the rubber wheels on the tiled floor.

Five feet from the door, she recognized his voice. "...been a little overwhelmed with the baby and everything at home."

She drew to a stop. He was talking about her.

Was he *complaining* about her?

There was a throaty, feminine chuckle. "I have a hard time imagining that. Never been married."

She even sounded pretty. Why couldn't the new vice principal have had an annoying high-pitched Minnie Mouse voice or something?

*Go home.* Nothing good was going to come from this. Already, hurt was surging through her.

"I've been trying to pick up the slack, but—"

A human-sized shadow moved into the doorway. Maddox. She'd recognize those shoulders anywhere. He wasn't looking out into the hallway. Yet.

*Escape.*

But she was frozen in place. Her skin felt scraped raw. Her heartbeat was pounding in her ears.

She must've made some movement, because his head turned. And then she was pinned in place, like a butterfly stabbed to a piece of paper.

"Haley? What're you—?"

She fixed a bright smile in place, as if she hadn't been skulking out in the darkened hallway. As if she hadn't just heard what she had.

"I was in town for Elijah's doctor's appointment,

and I thought I'd stop by and surprise you." Had that been her voice? Syrupy sweet and almost obnoxious? Tone it down, or he'd know something was wrong. "You weren't in your classroom, and I saw the light on down here..."

The hallway lights came on with a snap of fluorescent bulbs. She blinked against the brightness.

When she could focus again, Maddox was there, folding her into an embrace.

Could he feel how tense she was?

Over his shoulder, a woman had exited the lounge and stood waiting.

She wasn't pretty. She was *gorgeous*. A straight fall of light blonde hair just touched the tops of her shoulders. She was slim—no mommy-tummy on this one—and stylish, wearing a white button-down blouse tucked into a charcoal pencil skirt. And Louboutins.

Haley hadn't seen Louboutins since she'd left the city. Who would wear them in an empty building during summer break?

A homewrecker, that's who. Someone trying to make an impression.

She couldn't seem to grasp her composure as Maddox let her go.

He didn't seem to notice anything was amiss.

"This is Kiera Martin, the new VP. Kiera, my wife Haley."

He didn't sound upset that she'd barged in. He sounded proud. Of her?

She didn't know what to think as Kiera Martin took two svelte steps forward, her hand outstretched. "Hi, there."

She had a firm handshake, and unless Haley was mistaken, her gaze was assessing. Then her eyes fell to the stroller.

"And this must be the little man."

Haley had to clear her throat to get the words out. "This is Elijah."

Kiera Martin squatted in front of the stroller, cooing. The movement should've been awkward in her slim skirt, but she made even that look elegant.

Haley had never felt so frumpy as she did right this moment, still in her maternity jeans and a too-large T-shirt.

Haley tried to squelch the ugly emotions running rampant inside her, but it wasn't happening.

Maddox's arm came around her waist. "I was just rinsing out the coffee pot before I headed home. It was a two-pot kind of day."

That was his excuse, huh?

And what had School Administrator Barbie been doing in there?

Flirting, probably.

Haley's smile wobbled. "Elijah and I won't keep you."

Maddox squeezed her, still oblivious to her tension. "I'm done for the day. Catch you later, Kiera."

"Goodbye."

He let go of Haley to grab the handles of the stroller, leaving her to walk beside him. She couldn't help taking one more glance behind her.

Kiera Martin stood watching them, an expression Haley couldn't read on her face.

# CHAPTER 6

*W*hy was the dog whining in the middle of the night?

Haley was half-asleep, warm and ready for her bed after feeding and snuggling Elijah in the rocking chair in his room.

But as she stepped into the hallway, she heard Livy's puppy whining through the girl's closed door.

So far, Livy had kept her word. She'd fed the puppy, exercised it, played with it, and taken it outside, even during the night.

Had Livy somehow slept through its whining?

Elijah was such a light sleeper that Haley didn't dare let the dog keep making noise.

She cracked the bedroom door. "Livy," she whispered. "Wake up."

There was no movement from the girl in the bed, but the puppy set to scratching. And barked.

"Ssh," Haley shushed it, stepping into the room. "Livy." How was the girl sleeping through this?

Maybe it would've been kinder to simply take the dog out, but Haley didn't feel kind. She walked to the bed and reached for Livy's foot, buried under the quilt. A soft shake might wake the girl.

Except her fingers met only blankets and more blankets.

Stomach pinching in instant worry, she stepped back to the door and slapped on the overhead light.

Livy's bed was empty.

She rushed into the hall and then into the master bedroom, calling for Maddox.

By the time she got the light on, he was sitting up in bed, bare-chested and squinting against the light.

"What's going on?"

"Livy's gone. She's not in her bed."

He reacted instantly, standing and reaching for the T-shirt on top of his dresser. He squinted at the clock. It was after two.

"Try her cell phone," he said as he headed to their en suite bathroom.

Good idea. Her hands shook as she grabbed her phone from its charger on the nightstand. She hadn't thought beyond *get Maddox*. Even now, she was so panicked she couldn't marshal her thoughts.

She dialed Livy.

And heard the girl's phone ring from down the hall.

The dog barked again, but for once, Elijah waking up was the least of Haley's worries.

She hung up.

Maddox must've heard the phone ring, too, because his face was grim when exited the bathroom. He reached for the boots at the end of the bed.

"Should I call some of her friends?" Haley asked, half to herself. She headed for the door, intending to grab Livy's phone.

"Hang on." Maddox had one boot on. "Let's think a little before we put out an all-points bulletin."

He sounded to calm and she felt anything but.

"Justin and Katie used to sneak out and head down to the pond sometimes. Or the barn. She might not be out with someone. Maybe she's on the property."

Haley's head started to pound. "She hasn't wanted to spend time in the barn in months. And alone? Why would she do that?"

He shrugged as he pulled on his other boot. "Why do kids push the limits? Break the rules? Because they can."

He might be happy to stay calm and start with the barn, but Haley was going to get that phone and make some calls. If Livy's friends gave her a hard time afterward, so be it.

She started down the hall, Maddox following more slowly. She wracked her brain, trying to remember the name of the new girl in town that Livy had been spending some time with. Did she have an older brother? Or was that another one of Livy's friends? Baby brain and pure exhaustion made it so difficult to pull on the right strings in her brain.

She was muttering to herself. The dog barked again.

"Do you want me to take the puppy out?" Maddox asked from behind her.

"Do what you want," she mumbled. "It's what you've been doing all summer anyway."

She closed her eyes, suffering a beat of anguish at the words she hadn't meant to say.

And then Maddox had her arm in a firm grip and swung her around to face him. "You wanna run that by me again?"

Frustration and anger peaked, and she blurted it all out. "You decided to teach this summer without even asking my opinion." And he was spending time during the day with a lovely, enchanting new woman. "You bought the puppy. You want to handle Livy *your* way."

He shook his head, his expression disbelieving. Maybe wondering why she was picking the fight right now.

But behind that, she also saw a hint of guilt.

And that broke her. Tears welled in her eyes.

"Please tell me you're not having an affair with Kiera Martin."

He wouldn't have looked more shocked if she'd slapped him.

He opened his mouth. Closed it. Opened it again.

Before he could say anything—would she believe him if he'd denied it?—a ding from Livy's room interrupted. A notification.

MADDOX HAD BEEN RIGHT about Livy.

He found her sleeping on a soft bed of hay, her sweatshirt wadded up beneath her head, in a stall with Dolly. The mare had been Katie's horse and was in her last days. Her muzzle was flecked with white. The gentle animal slept beside the girl.

He'd never felt so upside-down about being right.

What Haley had said...

He still felt breathless with the hurt of it.

The notification from Livy's phone had interrupted their conversation—fight?—but had turned out to be a friend's post on some app called Instagram. Nothing related to his teenager. Whom he wanted to talk to about having her phone on at night. Later.

He'd headed for the barn without another word —too afraid to say the wrong thing and have things between him and Haley blow up even worse.

How could she think that?

That's maybe what hurt the most. That Haley had so little faith in him.

A relationship with Kiera had never even occurred to him. She was nice, maybe a little too chatty, but that was it.

He loved *Haley*. Loved their family. He was getting up every day at oh-dark-thirty to prove it, doing laundry and dishes like a madman.

For the first time since before they'd married, he wondered if he could be enough for her.

The thoughts swirling around in his head became too heavy for him to bear. He leaned one hand against the stall wall. Hung his head.

The voice in his head started to sound an awful lot like his dad's.

Maddox hadn't been enough to keep Justin and Katie in line when they'd been teenagers and his mom had fallen into depression. He hadn't been enough to keep Justin from his womanizing or from spiraling into depression after his bull-riding accident. He hadn't been enough for Livy when his little girl had grieved for her mother and father, not until Haley had come along.

What made him think he could be husband enough to Haley?

She was in a tough place, with the baby stealing her sleep and demanding care. He didn't begrudge her the need for help or the distance between them, distance she'd created. He'd thought they'd ride these difficult few months out together. But this—

He didn't know if there was a way to move past the accusation she'd leveled at him.

Katie stirred in the hay and murmured in her sleep, bringing him out of his thoughts and back into the present.

Not Katie. Livy.

For a moment, with his emotions all over the place, he'd seen his sister and not the niece that he loved like a daughter.

Katie'd left him with a job to do. And maybe he had been acting the pushover lately. Had he?

That ended now.

"Wake up," he said, breaking the suffocating silence.

Livy stirred and then bolted upright into a sitting position. She took one look at him and grimaced.

"Oh, crap."

"*Oh crap* is right. Your puppy was whining. Do you know worried Haley was when she found you missing?"

He blocked off the part of his insides that howled just at the thought of his wife. He couldn't deal with it now.

Livy brushed her hair out of her face, knocked some straw off her bent knee. "I fell asleep."

Obviously.

She wrapped her arms around her bent knees, huddled in on herself.

"Why'd you sneak out in the first place? You were already grounded. You know things are going to get ten times worse for you, right?"

Her lips tightened into a white line, she turned her face away to look at the horse. Shutting him out.

He was about done with the women in his life closing the door to him.

"Livy?" he prodded, but still got nothing. "This is not like you. The last month or so you've gone off the deep end. I need you to tell me what's up."

Where had his sweet girl gone? Was she still in there somewhere?

She stayed silent, with that mulish jut of her chin.

And everything that had happened since he'd been woken from a deep sleep converged, and he lost his temper.

"Fine." He pushed away from the wall and stood straight. "You promised me you were going to take care of the dog, and you broke your word on that. Maybe the puppy was a mistake." He pivoted and marched toward the barn door.

She jumped up and ran out of the stall on his heels. "Uncle Maddox, no. I've been taking care of Sadie. Every day and every night."

"Not tonight." He strode for the barn door.

"You can't take her away. That's not fair!"

Her wail split the quiet night air as they emerged into humid darkness. The sky was a midnight canvas with twinkling stars strewn across it, glorious and beautiful.

Or it would've been, if he had the capacity to feel anything other than numb.

"Life's not fair," he said. "We don't have a three-strikes rule here. You were already grounded, and you snuck out again. You broke our trust—my trust."

"You can't take her away! Uncle Maddox, please!"

He didn't answer, even as her heartbroken plea pierced his heart. She was really worked up.

"You'd better keep your voice down," he warned as his boots hit the porch. She was still following him. "If you wake up the baby, Haley'll have your hide."

He felt the change in the air when she stopped following him.

He glanced over his shoulder to see her on the top step.

"I hate you," she cried out. And took off into the dark night.

# CHAPTER 7

*M*addox sat on the porch steps, his empty coffee mug dangling from his hand.

It was almost nine a.m., and Livy still hadn't come back.

He'd called Mrs. Heller, who'd agreed to cover for him this morning. He hated letting his boss down, but this couldn't wait. His family was more important than his job.

He'd never gone back to sleep, choosing to recline on the living room couch and wait for his daughter. Who'd never shown.

She'd probably gone back to the barn. Maybe curled up in the rickety treehouse he and Justin had built twenty-some years ago. He knew she hadn't called anyone to pick her up, because her phone was still upstairs. And if she'd decided to hitchhike, one of his neighbors was sure to give him a call.

Which meant she was still on the property. Likely getting hungry.

And probably still angry.

His anger had faded to a dull ache behind his breastbone—like a linebacker had bruised his ribs, only there was no purple skin.

He didn't know how to heal what was wrong with him.

Haley had left for some appointment a half hour ago, leaving Elijah upstairs sleeping.

She hadn't looked him in the eyes in the few seconds she'd gathered her purse and keys before she'd run out the door.

Was she really going to pretend that the words she'd said last night had never been uttered? Because that wasn't going to fly with him.

He'd given her time. He'd given her space. He'd hoped that being there for her was going to be enough.

But if it wasn't, then he was done playing nice. They were going to have words, and he was going to fix this. Fix all of it.

He just had to figure out how.

His resolve flickered when Livy crept past the edge of the barn.

He saw when she caught sight of him, how her posture changed, her spine going rigid.

But she approached, if a little wary.

When she got close, he patted the top step next to him. She hesitated. He picked up the overstuffed breakfast burrito he'd wrapped in a paper towel and offered it to her.

She sat down beside him. She unwrapped the food, but didn't start eating immediately.

"I want to go live with Uncle Justin and Aunt Valri." She said the words while staring at her boots.

He absorbed them like the punch they were. "No way." His reaction was swift and sure. "That's not gonna happen."

He saw her jaw shift to the side, saw the quick blink of her eyes, as if she were fighting tears.

He put his arm around her shoulders. Teenager or not, she was still his little girl. "Just because we have one fight doesn't mean we give up on each other."

She shifted, but he didn't let go of her. He wasn't walking away from her—from either of his girls.

"Talk to me. Is something going on with one of your friends? Some boy you haven't told me about?"

She was silent, shook her head.

That would've been too easy.

"Is it about Elijah? I know Haley's been busy with

him—I have too. You haven't been wanting to hold him as much lately."

A single tear slipped down her cheek. Oh, she was breaking his heart now.

She sniffed. "It's not that." She rubbed her cheek on her shoulder, removing all traces of that tear. "It's... mom. Sort of. I don't know how to explain it..."

He waited for a few beats. When she didn't keep going, he said, "Try."

She started out at the barn, squinting. "It sounds stupid. Dolly is like... really old. In horse years."

He knew. The old gal was having a hard time getting around.

"And when she"—here came another sniffle —"dies, it'll be like the last link to my mom is... gone."

Oh, Livy.

He didn't wait to see if she started crying. He gave a good tug and brought her head to rest on his shoulder, tucking her in tight like he would've when she was small.

"What am I, chopped liver?" he asked, brushing a kiss on the top of her head.

She exhaled a huff. "I told you it was stupid."

"It's not stupid."

She leaned on him, quiet for moments. She'd been sneaking out to the barn to see her mom's horse. Not to party. Or even hang out with friends.

"I wish you'd told me sooner. You're going through a new stage of life. It's natural to miss your mom."

She nodded, her head nudging his shoulder.

"Wait a minute. Lately you've been avoiding the barn. Complaining about your chores and doing your best to stay away during the day."

She shrugged, straightened up. He let his arm fall away. Apparently, the time limit for comforting his teenaged daughter was over.

She took a bite of burrito. Chewed. "Sometimes it really hurts to go in there. You know?"

He nodded. "And at night?"

She swallowed hard. "I don't want her to be alone. If it's her time, y'know?" Her voice wobbled at the end.

He bumped her shoulder with his. She kept eating.

"If you'd told me, we could've taken turns."

"Nuh-uh," she mumbled, mouth full. She swallowed. "You're already helping Haley with everything. And the baby..."

He shrugged. "We're family. We'll figure it out."

He only hoped they could.

HALEY'S KNEES knocked as she walked through the library stacks to the conference room.

She hadn't planned to come to the support group meeting, but after last night, something had to give.

Maddox hadn't come back to bed. He'd texted her that he'd found Livy.

He hadn't said a word to her this morning as she'd left. It was obvious he was still angry.

She didn't want to be right about her suspicions.

People didn't just jump into affairs. Kiera Martin was new in town. There wouldn't have been time for something to develop, would there?

But Maddox hadn't denied it.

And she couldn't forget that tiny spark of guilt she'd seen on his face last night. He was keeping something from her.

Why hadn't he denied it?

Tears threatened, and she gave a valiant sniff, turned her head so an older man browsing the mystery section wouldn't see her trying not to cry.

She had to get ahold of herself.

How was she supposed to go into this conference room and fake like she was a good mom? She was barely holding herself together.

She dawdled outside the big wooden door until a hand touched her elbow.

"Are you here for the support group? C'mon in."

A woman a few years older than she was gave her a smile and looked as if she wouldn't take no for an answer as she ushered Haley inside the room. There were nine or ten other women inside, sipping coffee and chatting. Some sat in chairs surrounding the long conference table while several loitered around a box of donuts and the coffee pot on a smaller table on the side wall.

She recognized Dana Peterson, a mother with two small children, from church. Everyone else was a stranger to her.

Maybe she didn't belong here, either.

But before she could turn and bolt, the woman who'd followed her into the room said, "Welcome, everyone. Ready to get started?"

And one woman was pressing a napkin-wrapped glazed donut into Haley's hand. Another patted the open seat beside her, beckoning Haley to sit.

She did.

Around the room, other women settled into chairs, getting comfortable.

The speaker introduced herself as Sally Phillips. A mom of four whose son A.J. had just turned two. She'd been the instigator of the group eight years ago, when her first daughter had been born.

And then she looked right at Haley, whose face

grew hot. "We've got a new face today. Care to intro-
duce yourself? Tell us about your little one."

She hid her shaking hands in her lap. "Oh, um,
okay. I'm Haley Michaels, and my son Elijah just
passed six months."

Should she say more? Mention she was married?
Tell them about Livy?

Before she could get her thoughts in order, Sally
smiled warmly. "Welcome."

Everyone around the table murmured their
welcomes too, smiling and nodding as if they were
happy she was here.

Was that it? She breathed a sigh of relief that she
could sit back and listen for now.

Sally gestured to one of the women on the far
side of the table. "Candy, last time we met, you
mentioned little Myron's acid reflux. Do you have an
update for us?"

One by one, the women around the table talked
about the struggles they were going through. Sometimes the group had suggestions for them. Sometimes the room remained silent as everyone just
listened.

"We've tried the medicine and it seems to be
helping, but every time Silas nurses, he spits up at
least half of what he's eaten. It seems like he's hungry
all the time and I'm not sure my milk supply is

KISSED BY A COWBOY - THE SEQUEL

keeping up. This morning he spit up all over my favorite blouse. I was going to wear it today, and I started bawling. I couldn't help it."

Another woman shared, "We never should've graduated Avery to the big girl bed. *Every single night* she's climbing into bed with my husband and me. I try to send her back, but he just lets her climb over him and get right in the middle of us. I can't sleep with her kicking and rolling over every ten minutes."

From the far side of the table: "My husband wants to go on a Caribbean cruise this summer. He doesn't get that I can't seem to shed the last thirty pounds of baby weight. After three kids, I hate the way I look in a bathing suit. But I can't tell him that I don't want to go on vacation."

"Every single one of the kids Sammy Junior's age are crawling," said a worried-looking mom to Haley's left. "Every kid in his daycare group. My sister's kid. Everyone. And he just lays there, watching. I've tried coaxing him, showing him how to do it, everything! I've talked to his pediatrician, and he says Sammy will crawl when he's ready. But I'm afraid there's something wrong with him."

As each woman around the table spoke, Haley began to get more and more choked up.

Finally, Sally looked right at her. "Haley, is there

anything you'd like us to know about you and Elijah?"

To her horror, she burst into noisy sobs. She covered her face with both hands, trying to calm down. Someone pushed a few Kleenexes into her palm, and she dabbed at her face. Drew a deep breath.

Tears were still rolling down her cheeks as she glanced around the table. "I was r-really scared to come here today. I thought for sure you all would see me and know how big a fraud I am as a mother. B-but y'all are frauds too!"

She hadn't meant to say it like that, but quiet giggles went around the table. Several heads nodded.

And that gave Haley the courage to share. "I th-thought Elijah would be sleeping through the night by now. He's up several times during the night."

"Honey, you gotta let him cry it out," said a woman from down the table. More nods.

Maybe she wouldn't screw up her kid after all.

"I k-keep thinking that if I could just sleep for eight hours—just once—I could get my head on straight. And maybe..." She inhaled deeply. "Maybe I'll stop being so afraid. Of everything. Of ruining his life. That he'll get hurt because of me. Or get sick and I'll do the wrong thing. That I'm a bad mother."

Saying the words made her eyes well with tears again.

She didn't know the woman sitting next to her, but the lady put her arm around Haley's shoulders.

Sally looked at her, eyes glazed with compassion. "I can pretty much guarantee that every single one of us has felt those same fears at some point."

Heads nodded around the table.

Sally went on. "I know when my oldest was born, I felt paralyzed by the same kind of fears you're talking about."

"What'd you do?" Haley asked softly. She was tired of feeling this way, balanced on the razor's edge, afraid of doing something wrong so that she did nothing.

"I kept doing what I was doing. I fed the baby, changed a couple thousand diapers, made dinner. And slowly, I found a way to take care of myself, too."

More nodding, this time with murmured assents from around the table.

Dana spoke up. "If you aren't taking care of yourself, you'll be no good to anyone. For me, finding this group and being able to talk about what I was going through was a huge help. I'm so thankful to all of you." She sniffed back tears.

Next to Dana, another woman spoke. "The fear

doesn't ever go away. But experience is life's teacher. You'll start to recognize those little fevers for what they are, and in turn you'll be able to identify when something major is wrong. There's nothing wrong with being a little over-protective while your son is still tiny. Call the doctor's office if you need to."

After that, the meeting started to break up. Several women, including Dana and Sally, walked over to hug her and encourage her.

And as she left, she realized that she wasn't alone.

She'd felt alone in her fears all this time. Was it really as easy as sharing them?

Why hadn't she shared them with Maddox?

Oh, dear Lord. What had she done? Last night, her hurtful words.

She had to find a way to apologize.

MADDOX AND LIVY were making ice cream when Haley walked into the kitchen. The restaurant-grade ice cream machine was whirring noisily, and for a moment, she experienced a surge of worry for Elijah. Would they be able to hear him if he cried from upstairs—?

And then she saw the video baby monitor sitting on the counter. On the screen, her son was sleeping peacefully, one thumb stuck in his mouth.

Livy was wiping down what looked like strawberry juice and seeds from the counter. A pile of strawberries waited on the counter, a paring knife lying beside the cutting board.

Maddox looked up from the sink, where he was scrubbing out a pot. His gaze met hers, and she saw instantly how very wounded he was.

She'd done that to him.

She swallowed hard. "Can I help?"

Livy looked shocked as she tossed a dirty paper towel into the trash.

Had it really been that long since she'd initiated time spent with her girl? That was another arrow to the heart.

"We're pretty much done," Maddox said. His words hit her like a blow.

He meant with the ice cream, she told herself. Not their relationship.

But her chest still felt tight. It was hard to breathe. She looked down at the floor to gather herself.

Livy's puppy had been chewing mightily on a rope toy beneath the kitchen table. As Haley's gaze flicked to her, the dog perked up her head, ears flicking.

She squatted. Clapped her hands. "C'mere, girl."

The puppy got up and stumbled over its own feet

before it scrabbled across the floor to her. Haley picked it up, cuddling it. Holding it for the first time. She stood, holding the puppy against her chest.

Livy's eyes had gone wide.

Maddox's expression was inscrutable as the puppy licked her chin. She rubbed one hand along its back, soothing it.

She needed to do this. "I need to apologize to you, Livy." She tried to send Maddox a mental message from across the room. *And you. I'm so sorry!*

Livy's nose wrinkled. "For what?"

"I haven't been doing a very good job as your mom."

The puppy wriggled, and Haley set her down on the floor. She didn't go back to the rope but rushed into the living room with a soft bark.

"She's really cute," she told Livy. Then, "Elijah has needed me so much, and I haven't... it's been really hard to adjust to how things are now. I should've been paying more attention to you and your needs. And I'm sorry."

Her throat closed up as she spoke the last words.

Maddox abandoned his pot. He stood silently at the counter, wiping his hands with a dish towel.

But it was Livy she couldn't look away from. The teen's face crumpled, and she rushed forward for Haley to catch in a full-body hug.

"I'm sorry, too," Livy murmured, not letting go. "I shouldn't have snuck out. D-dad says I can't keep Sadie because I broke the rules."

Ouch. Livy wasn't blaming him, though. She'd said *Dad.*

"That seems a little harsh," she said. "Coming from someone like your dad. I think we should keep Sadie."

"Really?" Livy leaned back in her arms, looking hopefully from Haley to Maddox and back again.

Maddox's expression hadn't changed. He crossed his arms over his chest. "First I'm a pushover and now I'm too harsh?"

"You're perfect!" Livy cried. She threw herself into his arms, and he caught her in a hug.

But over the girl's head, his expression was drawn.

The over timer went off, and Livy sprang away from her uncle. "The cookies are ready!"

"Cookies *and* ice cream?" Haley teased.

"And Dad doesn't have to go to work until after lunch."

Haley glanced his way again, but his stony expression remained.

She'd hurt him. Badly. And she needed to fix it. But Livy needed her too, as evidenced by the way the girl took her hand and dragged her to the oven.

"I thought we could make ice cream sandwiches. The ice cream needs another ten minutes, which is just long enough for the cookies to cool."

And of course Elijah chose that moment to wake up.

She went upstairs, and the baby grinned widely when she reached into the crib to pick him up. His grin revealed a perfect white tooth on his bottom gum.

# CHAPTER 8

$\mathcal{M}$ addox's grace from Mrs. Heller ran out, and he had to return to teach the last two hours of the day.

The kids were antsy and cranky. He felt the same way.

Only, his frustrations didn't stem from a long summer day indoors, learning math and history.

Something had changed in Haley between the time she'd walked out of the house and when she'd returned. She'd been back to the quietly joyous woman he'd known and loved before Elijah had come along and disturbed the balance of their family.

Was it wrong that he'd wanted to be the one to help her find her new normal?

They still had unresolved issues. But they hadn't

had a chance to talk, not with Elijah gurgling happily from his high chair and Livy chattering like her old self.

The dismissal bell rang, and his kids cleared out in under a minute. It was the work of ten minutes to straighten up the classroom and chart Monday's lesson plan on the chalkboard.

He was pulling the strap of his messenger bag over his shoulder when Kiera knocked at the doorway.

He winced, hoping she didn't catch it. He tried to cover, fumbling in his pocket for his keys. It wasn't her fault that his marriage was on the rocks.

"Rough day?" she asked.

He shrugged. No way was he airing his personal problems with her.

"I came by to check on you... on your class earlier and noticed Mrs. Heller was in here. Is everything okay?"

"We had some stuff going on at home. It's fine now." Or it would be, once he got a chance to really sit down and talk with Haley.

He started for the door but stopped abruptly when she reached out and touched his upper arm. He took a step back.

She didn't seem to register his discomfort. Her smile was warm and friendly. "I was wondering... Do you think you'd want to grab a coffee sometime? Maybe in that few weeks between the end of summer school and meet-the-teacher day?"

He was instantly flummoxed. "What for?" He winced. That might not have been the most polite way to ask. She wasn't his boss, but it was a general rule that you didn't want to get on the bad side of anyone in administration.

She tilted her head to one side, smiling. She wasn't flirting with him. Was she? "I'm new in town, and I wouldn't mind making some new friends. And we could talk shop, too. Maybe you can tell me the teachers to steer clear of."

Mind whirling, he replayed every moment of the time he'd spent in her company since she'd arrived during the second week of summer school. He'd helped her move some furniture for her office. Greeted her and made small talk in the teachers' lounge. He couldn't think of one instance where he'd shown more than a co-worker level of interest in Kiera.

He'd been friendly. That was it.

But first, Haley had had her suspicions. And now this.

Was it possible he was giving off some kind of flirtatious vibe without even knowing it?

He'd have to figure that out later. He cleared his

throat. "Listen, Kiera. I am a happily married man. I haven't had to invoke a rule like *no coffee or lunch alone with a female coworker* before, but the truth is, I don't think my wife would be okay with that. I respect my wife and I would never do anything to hurt her. Not even the hint of anything that might hurt her. So, no, I won't be able to go to coffee with you."

Her smile faded at his blunt response. He saw color climbing into her cheeks, but he also knew that staying in this room, alone with her, might be enough to cause him problems, if she decided to get annoyed, and petty. If she lied to the principal or superintendent. If she said *he'd* come on to *her*.

"I gotta go," he said and brushed by her quickly.

He didn't sit in his truck in the parking lot, either. His brain was on fire trying to make sense of last night and what had just happened.

It was coincidence that the very thing Haley had been afraid of had happened. Wasn't it?

He hit the gas pedal hard on his way out of town. He'd been blunt with Kiera. And now, he needed to talk to his wife. The time for distance, for tiptoeing around each other, was over.

They were going to hash this out tonight.

# CHAPTER 9

$\mathcal{U}$nlike the evening Maddox and Livy had come home late to a cold supper, tonight the back door banged open while Haley was still getting dressed.

She paused in front of the mirror, one earring dangling from her lobe. She only had on her bra and panties. Because she was alone in the house.

There were only a couple people who felt comfortable enough to barge into her house.

"Haley?" Maddox called out.

She grabbed the robe from the foot of the bed and donned it, quickly tying the sash. She stuck her head into the hallway. "Upstairs!"

He wasn't wasting any time. His tread on the stairs was sure and swift.

She pulled a face at herself in the mirror. Old

ratty robe and one earring. So much for the impression she'd wanted to make tonight.

"Something smells good down there—" He cut himself off. Stopped in the doorway, taking her in. "You're wearing makeup again."

She tried not to flush at his scrutiny. She really did. Not that it helped, she thought as heat crept into her face.

"It's chicken Parmesan," she said. "Dinner will be ready in about an hour."

He lifted the strap of his messenger bag—the one she'd bought him just before he'd started teaching—over his head and deposited it on his side of the bed.

"Special occasion?" he asked. He wasn't looking directly at her anymore, but he didn't seem as stony-faced as he'd been earlier in the kitchen, and she felt a surge of hope. Maybe she could still fix this.

"I hope so," she whispered. She was opening her mouth to tell him how sorry she was when he sat on the end of the bed and put his face in his hands.

Her stomach did a slow somersault. "M-Maddox?"

She started to cross to him but stopped when he said, "You were right."

Everything froze around her. It felt as if even her heart stopped. But no—there was a slow, deafening thump in her eardrums. Her heartbeat.

KISSED BY A COWBOY - THE SEQUEL

Funny how it could keep beating when she felt as if the world she'd known had just imploded.

He rubbed his hands down his face and then clasped his fingers together, resting his elbows on his thighs. He looked up at her, eyes devastated. "At least, you were part right."

He went on to detail the afternoon's events for her.

Relief coursed through her, so deep that she sagged onto the corner of the bed, two feet still separating them. Limp, but relieved.

"I haven't sought her out in any way," he said, his gaze direct and unflinching. "I haven't flirted or given her any sign, unless... Do you think I'm a flirt, in general? All the time?"

His direct gaze asked for the truth, and how could she deny it to him?

"No." She had to clear her throat because the denial that had emerged was barely audible. "No," she said more strongly. "You're not. I didn't actually mean what I said last night."

She saw his own relief cross his expression. Knew how very badly she'd hurt him. She ducked her head.

And because her head was bent, she saw him extend his hand on the bedspread, palm upward.

She slipped her hand into his.

"Why'd you say it, then?" he asked quietly.

Could she tell him all of it? Trust him with all of it?

"No more hiding from me," he said.

Of course, she could.

"There's some stuff with Elijah that we should talk about later." There. She'd started with the easy part. But this... She forced the words out. "Mostly, I said it because I know I can't compare to someone like her, not anymore."

He tapped his thumb on the back of her hand, and she looked up into his dear face. He looked baffled. "What are you talking about?"

Knees knocking, she stood. He let go of her hand, and she tugged on the knot of the robe. "I was going to put on a dress, but..." She let the robe fall open, revealing her greatest insecurity to him. No one could blame her if she scrunched her eyes closed. "I look so... ugly." The word punched out of her on a soft sob, but she reined in her emotions tightly. This wasn't the time for breaking down.

Instantly, he was there, closing her in his arms, pressing kisses against her jaw. "What are you talking about? You're beautiful. Gorgeous. I—"

She shook her head, denying his words even as hearing them pressed all her hope buttons. He couldn't really think that.

"My body is..." She shook her head, unable to put it into words. The extra pounds, the stretch marks, the blotches on her skin.

She would never look the way she had before.

One of his hands came inside her robe to rest on her bare hip. "This body?" he asked. His nose touched the sensitive place behind her ear, and she shivered. She couldn't help it.

"This body that bore my son?"

She nodded, still pressing her eyes tightly closed.

"Haley, I love your body." His thumb ran up her side, as if punctuating his words. "I love how we fit together so perfectly." He kissed the base of her neck, his other hand pulling her even closer. "I'll never stop wanting you."

He kissed her lips then, his mouth teasing and caressing until her head swam.

Until she ached to believe him.

He broke the kiss, breathing hard and pressing his jaw to her temple. "Where are the kids?"

She was panting just as hard as he was. "Ryan and Ash's. For a few hours, at least."

His eyes lit with a lazy heat. "Good."


DINNER WAS SLIGHTLY BURNT. And Maddox couldn't care less.

"I love you," Haley said quietly over her plate of chicken Parm.

She'd foregone the dress in favor of comfy sweatpants and a clean T-shirt—only when he'd insisted. He'd matched her outfit, as they'd been rushing to get dressed while the annoying kitchen timer beeped and beeped and beeped.

Now they were sitting cross-legged on the living room floor, both on the same side of the coffee table but facing each other as they chowed down.

He couldn't quit touching her. Right now, his foot brushed her thigh.

He wouldn't let her image issues get the better of her again. Trying to give her space had been the wrong answer. If the right answer was his constant affection, sneaking more kisses and cuddles, well, he'd fall on that grenade if he must.

He grinned.

She blushed adorably and shook her head, spooning another bite of food into her mouth. She chewed and swallowed. "I might've missed a few days of telling you, so I guess I'll have to catch up. I love you."

"I don't think I'll ever get tired of hearing that."

As she'd plated their supper, she'd told him about her fears for Elijah, her fear that she was a terrible mother. And she told him about the moms' support group. He was happy she'd found the women who could help, but he'd also been frustrated that she'd kept so much from him.

She'd promised to work on it, and that was all he could ask for.

All in all, his life had turned a one-eighty in the last twenty-four hours.

He didn't kid himself that things were going to be perfect from now on, but he felt confident that they could find a way forward.

She dawdled over the last two bites of food on her plate, playing with her fork. "Can I ask you something?"

"Anything."

"Last night, when we were fighting..."

He frowned. Hadn't they resolved everything stemming from last night?

"...it felt like there was something you were holding back."

Summer school. Cancun.

He sighed. "There is something." There was nothing for it now. She'd shared her hurts and fears tonight. He couldn't keep his secret any longer.

Her expression shuttered. She put her mostly-empty plate on the coffee table.

He dug his toe into her side, tickling her. "It's nothing bad."

She glanced up at him warily.

"I took on the summer school session because..." He paused for effect. "Because I booked a trip for us. The two of us. Cancun over Christmas break."

Her eyes lit up, but then her maternal caution overrode the excitement. "But what about—"

"The kids will be fine," he said, anticipating her refusal. "Elijah should be weaned by then—right?— and I already talked to Ryan and Ash. It'll only be for a few days, and it'll be good practice for them anyway."

She half-smiled at his veiled hint. "I already know. Ash told me last week."

He waggled his eyebrows. "So... we won't be gone on Christmas Day, I promise. It'll be good for us. A trip just the two of us. And with the extra money from me teaching the summer classes, it's already paid for."

She plunked her chin on one hand on the table's edge. "Your big secret wasn't nefarious after all."

"What do you take me for?" he teased.

"A pushover."

He narrowed his eyes in mock outrage. "This pushover *was* going to make you an ice cream sandwich, but not if you're gonna call names..."

She laughed, and he stood, holding out his hands to help her up.

She stood upright and then came into his arms easily.

He'd missed this. The easy connection between them. He didn't want to lose it ever again.

He rested one palm against her jaw. "I love you, wife. I'll never stop."

Her beautiful eyes filled with tears as she hugged him tightly. "Me either."

"I'm not sure I can do this," Haley said.

"Sure, you can." Maddox tangled their fingers together.

Overhead, the terminal PA system announced boarding for their flight.

She'd been fighting nerves all the way from Redbud Trails to the Oklahoma City airport, where they were supposed to be boarding a plane for Cancun. Right now.

She just didn't think she could step foot on it.

"What if something happens while we're gone?"

Maddox smiled patiently at her. "What if nothing happens?"

"Elijah—"

"Is fine," he countered.

They'd left both Livy and Elijah with Ryan and

Ashley last night in preparation for this early-morning flight.

"It's four days," her husband said. "Elijah and Livy will survive. And so will you."

How could he be so sure?

Passengers started trickling past the gate attendant and then disappearing down the jet bridge.

"We've come all the way," he coaxed. "You've planned and over-planned for the entire trip."

She might've gone a little overboard. She'd written a daily schedule for Elijah for each of the four days they'd be gone. And color-coded it.

And if Ashley didn't stick to the schedule, it wouldn't be the end of the world. Elijah was a happy, healthy baby. Four days of eating a little off-schedule and not sleeping enough wouldn't damage him.

Probably.

Over the past six months, she'd opened up to Maddox and her support group about the challenges —and wins—of caring for her son. Just talking about her fears had minimized most of them. She'd also had several appointments with a therapist and learned some coping techniques to help her deal with the more pervasive irrational fears—like that she'd accidentally bump the soft spot on his head or that they'd be in a car accident or that she'd drop him after his bath.

She knew her brand of mom-crazy was rearing its head right now. But she hadn't been away from Livy on an overnight trip in years. And she'd never been away from Elijah for more than a few hours.

Maddox leaned close to murmur in her ear. "Think about the couples massage we booked. And the beach, just waiting for you to arrive with your book in hand." He kissed the spot behind her ear. "And the great big king-size bed."

He was right. She needed to unplug, even if it felt painful at just this moment.

Clutching her ticket and passport in one hand and her husband in the other, she tugged him toward the gate attendant. "Come on, honey. Our vacation is waiting."

"That's my girl."

She was. Forever Maddox's girl.

Keeping Kayla

Melting Megan


COWBOY FAIRYTALES SERIES
(CONTEMPORARY ROMANCE)

Once Upon a Cowboy

Cowboy Charming

The Toad Prince

The Beastly Princess

The Lost Princess


HEART OF OKLAHOMA SERIES
(CONTEMPORARY ROMANCE)

Kissed by a Cowboy

Love Letters from Cowboy

Mistletoe Cowboy

Cowgirl for Keeps

Jingle Bell Cowgirl

Heart of a Cowgirl

3 Days with a Cowboy

Prodigal Cowgirl

## WYOMING LEGACY SERIES (HISTORICAL ROMANCE)

The Homesteader's Sweetheart

Roping the Wrangler

Return of the Cowboy Doctor

The Wrangler's Inconvenient Wife

A Cowboy for Christmas

Her Convenient Cowboy

Her Cowboy Deputy


## NOT IN A SERIES

How to Lose a Guy in 10 Dates

Santa Next Door

The Butterfly Bride

Secondhand Cowboy

Wagon Train Sweetheart (historical romance)

Made in the USA
Las Vegas, NV
05 June 2021

24242502R00152